MATILDA

"Funny, witty, fresh . . . Dahl at his outrageous best!"
—*The Baltimore Sun*

"Makes grown-ups wince and children beg for more."
—*Kirkus Reviews*

"A funny book with a child's perspective on an adult world. . . . Children will be waiting in line to read it."
—*School Library Journal,* starred review

"Dahl's best book yet."   —*Chicago Sun-Times*

"Roald Dahl has done it again. . . . Matilda will surely go straight to children's hearts."
—*The New York Times Book Review*

"A tour de force that kids will undoubtedly love."
—*The New Yorker*

PUFFIN BOOKS BY ROALD DAHL

Roald Dahl

MATILDA

Illustrations by Quentin Blake

PUFFIN BOOKS

For
Michael and Lucy

PUFFIN BOOKS
Published by the Penguin Group
Penguin Books USA Inc., 375 Hudson Street, New York, New York 10014, U.S.A.
Penguin Books Ltd, 27 Wrights Lane, London W8 5TZ, England
Penguin Books Australia Ltd, Ringwood, Victoria, Australia
Penguin Books Canada Ltd, 10 Alcorn Avenue, Toronto, Ontario, Canada M4V 3B2
Penguin Books (N.Z.) Ltd, 182–190 Wairau Road, Auckland 10, New Zealand
Penguin Books Ltd, Registered Offices: Harmondsworth, Middlesex, England

First published in Great Britain by Jonathan Cape Ltd., 1988
First published in the United States of America by Viking Penguin,
a division of Penguin Books USA Inc., 1988
Published in Puffin Books, 1990
This edition published in Puffin Books, 1996

1 3 5 7 9 10 8 6 4 2

Text copyright © Roald Dahl, 1988
Illustrations copyright © Quentin Blake, 1988
Cover art copyright © 1996 TriStar Pictures, Inc.
All rights reserved

Grateful acknowledgment is made for permission to reprint an excerpt from "In
Country Sleep" from *The Poems of Dylan Thomas*. Copyright 1947, 1952 Dylan
Thomas. Reprinted by permission of New Directions Publishing Corporation.

THE LIBRARY OF CONGRESS HAS CATALOGED THE PREVIOUS PUFFIN EDITION AS FOLLOWS:
Dahl, Roald. Matilda/Roald Dahl; illustrations by Quentin Blake. p. cm.
Reprint. Originally published: New York, N.Y.: Viking Kestrel, 1988.
Summary: Matilda applies her untapped mental powers to rid the school
of the evil, child-hating headmistress, Miss Trunchbull, and restore
her nice teacher, Miss Honey, to financial security.
[1. Schools—Fiction. 2. Humorous stories.] I. Blake, Quentin, ill. II. Title.
PZ7.D1515Mat 1990 [Fic]—dc20 89-10604
ISBN 0-14-03.4294-X

This edition ISBN 0-14-037985-1

Printed in the United States of America

Contents

The Reader of Books

It's a funny thing about mothers and fathers. Even when their own child is the most disgusting little blister you could ever imagine, they still think that he or she is wonderful.

Some parents go further. They become so blinded by adoration they manage to convince themselves their child has qualities of genius.

Well, there is nothing very wrong with all this. It's the way of the world. It is only when the parents begin telling *us* about the brilliance of their own revolting offspring, that we start shouting, "Bring us a basin! We're going to be sick!"

School teachers suffer a good deal from having to listen to this sort of twaddle from proud parents, but they usually get their own back when the time comes to write the end-of-term reports. If I were a teacher I would cook up some real scorchers for the children of doting parents. "Your son Maximilian", I would write, "is a total wash-out. I hope you have a family business you can push him into when he leaves school because he sure as heck won't get a job anywhere else." Or if I were feeling lyrical that day, I might write, "It is a curious truth that grasshoppers have their hearing-organs in the sides of the abdomen. Your daughter Vanessa, judging by what she's learnt this term, has no hearing-organs at all."

I might even delve deeper into natural history and say, "The periodical cicada spends six years as a grub underground, and no more than six *days* as a free creature of sunlight and air. Your son Wilfred has spent six years as a grub in this school and we are still waiting for him to emerge from the chrysalis." A particularly poisonous little girl might sting me into saying, "Fiona has the same glacial beauty as an iceberg, but unlike the iceberg she has absolutely nothing below the surface." I

think I might enjoy writing end-of-term reports for the stinkers in my class. But enough of that. We have to get on.

Occasionally one comes across parents who take the opposite line, who show no interest at all in their children, and these of course are far worse than the doting ones. Mr and Mrs Wormwood were two such parents. They had a son called Michael and a daughter called Matilda, and the parents looked upon Matilda in particular as nothing more than a scab. A scab is something you have to put up with until the time comes when you can pick it off and flick it away. Mr and Mrs Wormwood looked forward enormously to the time when they could pick their little daughter off and flick her away, preferably into the next county or even further than that.

It is bad enough when parents treat *ordinary* children as though they were scabs and bunions, but it becomes somehow a lot worse when the child in question is *extra*-ordinary, and by that I mean sensitive and brilliant. Matilda was both of these things, but above all she was brilliant. Her mind was so nimble and she was so quick to learn that her ability should have been obvious even to the most half-witted of parents. But Mr and Mrs Wormwood were both so gormless and so wrapped up in their own silly little lives that they failed to notice anything unusual about their daughter. To tell the truth, I doubt they would have noticed had she crawled into the house with a broken leg.

Matilda's brother Michael was a perfectly normal boy, but the sister, as I said, was something to make your eyes pop. By the age of *one and a half* her speech was perfect and she knew as many words as most grown-ups. The parents, instead of applauding her, called her a noisy chatterbox and told her sharply that small girls should be seen and not heard.

By the time she was *three*, Matilda had taught herself to read by studying newspapers and magazines that lay around the house. At the age of *four*, she could read fast and well and she naturally began hankering after books. The only book in the whole of this enlightened household was something called *Easy Cooking* belonging to her mother, and when she had read this from cover to cover and had learnt all the recipes by heart, she decided she wanted something more intcresting.

"Daddy," she said, "do you think you could buy me a book?"

"A *book*?" he said. "What d'you want a flaming book for?"

"To read, Daddy."

"What's wrong with the telly, for heaven's sake? We've got a lovely telly with a twelve-inch screen and now you come asking for a book! You're getting spoiled, my girl!"

Nearly every weekday afternoon Matilda was left alone in the house. Her brother (five years older than her) went to school. Her father went to work and her mother went out playing bingo in a town eight miles away. Mrs Wormwood was hooked on bingo and played it five afternoons a week. On the afternoon of the day when her father had refused to buy her a book, Matilda set out all by herself to walk to the public library in the village. When she arrived, she introduced herself to the librarian, Mrs Phelps. She asked if she might sit awhile and read a book. Mrs Phelps, slightly taken aback at the arrival of such a tiny girl unacccompanied by a parent, nevertheless told her she was very welcome.

"Where are the children's books please?" Matilda asked.

"They're over there on those lower shelves," Mrs Phelps told her. "Would you like me to help you find a nice one with lots of pictures in it?"

"No, thank you," Matilda said. "I'm sure I can manage."

From then on, every afternoon, as soon as her mother had left for bingo, Matilda would toddle down to the library. The walk took only ten minutes and this allowed her two glorious hours sitting quietly by herself in a cosy corner devouring one book after another. When she had read every single children's book in the place, she started wandering round in search of something else.

Mrs Phelps, who had been watching her with fascination for the past few weeks, now got up from her desk and went over to her. "Can I help you, Matilda?" she asked.

"I'm wondering what to read next," Matilda said. "I've finished all the children's books."

"You mean you've looked at the pictures?"

"Yes, but I've read the books as well."

Mrs Phelps looked down at Matilda from her great height and Matilda looked right back up at her.

"I thought some were very poor," Matilda said, "but others were lovely. I liked *The Secret Garden* best of all. It was full of mystery. The mystery of

13

the room behind the closed door and the mystery of the garden behind the big wall."

Mrs Phelps was stunned. "Exactly how old are you, Matilda?" she asked.

"Four years and three months," Matilda said.

Mrs Phelps was more stunned than ever, but she had the sense not to show it. "What sort of a book would you like to read next?" she asked.

Matilda said, "I would like a really good one that grown-ups read. A famous one. I don't know any names."

Mrs Phelps looked along the shelves, taking her time. She didn't quite know what to bring out. How, she asked herself, does one choose a famous grown-up book for a four-year-old girl? Her first thought was to pick a young teenager's romance of the kind that is written for fifteen-year-old schoolgirls, but for some reason she found herself instinctively walking past that particular shelf.

"Try this," she said at last. "It's very famous and very good. If it's too long for you, just let me know and I'll find something shorter and a bit easier."

"*Great Expectations*," Matilda read, "by Charles Dickens. I'd love to try it."

I must be mad, Mrs Phelps told herself, but to Matilda she said, "Of course you may try it."

Over the next few afternoons Mrs Phelps could hardly take her eyes from the small girl sitting for hour after hour in the big armchair at the far end of the room with the book on her lap. It was necessary to rest it on the lap because it was too heavy for her to hold up, which meant she had to sit leaning forward in order to read. And a strange sight it was, this tiny dark-haired person sitting there with her feet nowhere near touching the floor, totally absorbed in the wonderful adventures of Pip and old Miss Havisham and her cobwebbed house and by the spell of magic that Dickens the great story-teller had woven with his words. The only movement from the reader was the lifting of the hand every now and then to turn over a page, and Mrs Phelps always felt sad when the time came for her to cross the floor and say, "It's ten to five, Matilda."

During the first week of Matilda's visits Mrs Phelps had said to her, "Does your mother walk you down here every day and then take you home?"

"My mother goes to Aylesbury every afternoon to play bingo," Matilda had said. "She doesn't know I come here."

"But that's surely not right," Mrs Phelps said. "I think you'd better ask her."

"I'd rather not," Matilda said. "She doesn't encourage reading books. Nor does my father."

"But what do they expect you to do every afternoon in an empty house?"

"Just mooch around and watch the telly."

"I see."

"She doesn't really care what I do," Matilda said a little sadly.

Mrs Phelps was concerned about the child's safety on the walk through the fairly busy village High Street and the crossing of the road, but she decided not to interfere.

Within a week, Matilda had finished *Great Expectations* which in that edition contained four hundred and eleven pages. "I loved it," she said to Mrs Phelps. "Has Mr Dickens written any others?"

"A great number," said the astounded Mrs Phelps. "Shall I choose you another?"

Over the next six months, under Mrs Phelps's

watchful and compassionate eye, Matilda read the following books:

Nicholas Nickleby by Charles Dickens
Oliver Twist by Charles Dickens
Jane Eyre by Charlotte Brontë
Pride and Prejudice by Jane Austen
Tess of the D'Urbervilles by Thomas Hardy
Gone to Earth by Mary Webb
Kim by Rudyard Kipling
The Invisible Man by H. G. Wells
The Old Man and the Sea by Ernest Hemingway
The Sound and the Fury by William Faulkner
The Grapes of Wrath by John Steinbeck
The Good Companions by J. B. Priestley
Brighton Rock by Graham Greene
Animal Farm by George Orwell

It was a formidable list and by now Mrs Phelps was filled with wonder and excitement, but it was probably a good thing that she did not allow herself to be completely carried away by it all. Almost anyone else witnessing the achievements of this small child would have been tempted to make a great fuss and shout the news all over the village and beyond, but not so Mrs Phelps. She was someone who minded her own business and had long since discovered it was seldom worth while to interfere with other people's children.

"Mr Hemingway says a lot of things I don't understand," Matilda said to her. "Especially about men and women. But I loved it all the same. The

18

way he tells it I feel I am right there on the spot watching it all happen."

"A fine writer will always make you feel that," Mrs Phelps said. "And don't worry about the bits you can't understand. Sit back and allow the words to wash around you, like music."

"I will, I will."

"Did you know", Mrs Phelps said, "that public libraries like this allow you to borrow books and take them home?"

"I didn't know that," Matilda said. "Could *I* do it?"

"Of course," Mrs Phelps said. "When you have chosen the book you want, bring it to me so I can make a note of it and it's yours for two weeks. You can take more than one if you wish."

From then on, Matilda would visit the library only once a week in order to take out new books and return the old ones. Her own small bedroom now became her reading-room and there she would sit and read most afternoons, often with a mug of hot chocolate beside her. She was not quite tall enough to reach things around the kitchen, but she kept a small box in the outhouse which she brought in and stood on in order to get whatever she wanted. Mostly it was hot chocolate she made, warming the milk in a saucepan on the stove before mixing it. Occasionally she made Bovril or Ovaltine. It was pleasant to take a hot drink up to her room and have it beside her as she sat in her silent room reading in the empty house in the afternoons. The books transported her into new worlds and introduced her to amazing people who lived exciting lives. She went on olden-day sailing ships with Joseph Conrad. She went to Africa with Ernest Hemingway and to India with Rudyard Kipling. She travelled all over the world while sitting in her little room in an English village.

Mr Wormwood,
the Great Car Dealer

Matilda's parents owned quite a nice house with three bedrooms upstairs, while on the ground floor there was a dining-room and a living-room and a kitchen. Her father was a dealer in second-hand cars and it seemed he did pretty well at it.

"Sawdust", he would say proudly, "is one of the great secrets of my success. And it costs me nothing. I get it free from the sawmill."

"What do you use it for?" Matilda asked him.

"Ha!" the father said. "Wouldn't you like to know."

"I don't see how sawdust can help you to sell second-hand cars, daddy."

"That's because you're an ignorant little twit," the father said. His speech was never very delicate but Matilda was used to it. She also knew that he liked to boast and she would egg him on shamelessly.

"You must be very clever to find a use for something that costs nothing," she said. "I wish I could do it."

"You couldn't," the father said. "You're too stupid. But I don't mind telling young Mike here about it seeing he'll be joining me in the business one day." Ignoring Matilda, he turned to his son and said, "I'm always glad to buy a car when some fool has been crashing the gears so badly they're all worn out and rattle like mad. I get it cheap. Then all I do is mix a lot of sawdust with the oil in the gear-box and it runs as sweet as a nut."

"How long will it run like that before it starts rattling again?" Matilda asked him.

"Long enough for the buyer to get a good distance away," the father said, grinning. "About a hundred miles."

"But that's dishonest, daddy," Matilda said. "It's cheating."

"No one ever got rich being honest," the father said. "Customers are there to be diddled."

Mr Wormwood was a small ratty-looking man whose front teeth stuck out underneath a thin ratty moustache. He liked to wear jackets with large brightly-coloured checks and he sported ties that were usually yellow or pale green. "Now take mileage for instance," he went on. "Anyone who's buying a second-hand car, the first thing he wants to know is how many miles it's done. Right?"

"Right," the son said.

"So I buy an old dump that's got about a hundred and fifty thousand miles on the clock. I get it cheap. But no one's going to buy it with a mileage like that, are they? And these days you can't just take the speedometer out and fiddle the numbers back like you used to ten years ago. They've fixed it so it's impossible to tamper with it unless you're a ruddy watchmaker or something. So what do I do? I use my brains, laddie, that's what I do."

"How?" young Michael asked, fascinated. He

seemed to have inherited his father's love of crookery.

"I sit down and say to myself, how can I convert a mileage reading of one hundred and fifty thousand into only ten thousand without taking the speedometer to pieces? Well, if I were to run the car backwards for long enough then obviously that would do it. The numbers would click backwards, wouldn't they? But who's going to drive a flaming car in reverse for thousands and thousands of miles? You couldn't do it!"

"Of course you couldn't," young Michael said.

"So I scratch my head," the father said. "I use my brains. When you've been given a fine brain like I have, you've got to use it. And all of a sudden, the answer hits me. I tell you, I felt exactly like that other brilliant fellow must have felt when he discovered penicillin. 'Eureka!' I cried. 'I've got it!'"

"What did you do, dad?" the son asked him.

"The speedometer", Mr Wormwood said, "is run off a cable that is coupled up to one of the front wheels. So first I disconnect the cable where it joins the front wheel. Next, I get one of those high-speed electric drills and I couple that up to the end of the cable in such a way that when the drill turns, it turns the cable *backwards*. You got me so far? You following me?"

"Yes, daddy," young Michael said.

"These drills run at a tremendous speed," the father said, "so when I switch on the drill the mileage numbers on the speedo spin backwards at a fantastic rate. I can knock fifty thousand miles off the clock in a few minutes with my high-speed electric drill. And by the time I've finished, the car's only done ten thousand and it's ready for sale. 'She's almost new,' I say to the customer. 'She's hardly done ten thou. Belonged to an old lady who only used it once a week for shopping.'"

"Can you really turn the mileage back with an electric drill?" young Michael asked.

"I'm telling you trade secrets," the father said. "So don't you go talking about this to anyone else. You don't want me put in jug, do you?"

"I won't tell a soul," the boy said. "Do you do this to many cars, dad?"

"Every single car that comes through my hands gets the treatment," the father said. "They all have their mileage cut to under under ten thou before they're offered for sale. And to think I invented that all by myself," he added proudly. "It's made me a mint."

Matilda, who had been listening closely, said, "But daddy, that's even more dishonest than the sawdust. It's disgusting. You're cheating people who trust you."

"If you don't like it then don't eat the food in this house," the father said. "It's bought with the profits."

"It's dirty money," Matilda said. "I hate it."

Two red spots appears on the father's cheeks. "Who the heck do you think you are," he shouted, "The Archbishop of Canterbury or something, preaching to me about honesty? You're just an ignorant little squirt who hasn't the foggiest idea what you're talking about!"

"Quite right, Harry," the mother said. And to Matilda she said, "You've got a nerve talking to your father like that. Now keep your nasty mouth shut so we can all watch this programme in peace."

They were in the living-room eating their suppers on their knees in front of the telly. The suppers were TV dinners in floppy aluminium containers with separate compartments for the stewed meat,

the boiled potatoes and the peas. Mrs Wormwood sat munching her meal with her eyes glued to the American soap-opera on the screen. She was a large woman whose hair was dyed platinum blonde except where you could see the mousy-brown bits growing out from the roots. She wore heavy make-up and she had one of those unfortunate bulging figures where the flesh appears to be strapped in all around the body to prevent it from falling out.

"Mummy," Matilda said, "would you mind if I ate my supper in the dining-room so I could read my book?"

The father glanced up sharply. "*I* would mind!" he snapped. "Supper is a family gathering and no one leaves the table till it's over!"

"But we're not at the table," Matilda said. "We never are. We're always eating off our knees and watching the telly."

"What's wrong with watching the telly, may I ask?" the father said. His voice had suddenly become soft and dangerous.

Matilda didn't trust herself to answer him, so she kept quiet. She could feel the anger boiling up inside her. She knew it was wrong to hate her parents like this, but she was finding it very hard not to do so. All the reading she had done had given her a view of life that they had never seen. If only they would read a little Dickens or Kipling they would soon discover there was more to life than cheating people and watching television.

Another thing. She resented being told constantly that she was ignorant and stupid when she knew she wasn't. The anger inside her went on boiling and boiling, and as she lay in bed that night she made a decision. She decided that every time her father or her mother was beastly to her, she would get her own back in some way or another. A small victory or two would help her to tolerate their idiocies and would stop her from going crazy. You must remember that she was still hardly five years old and it is not easy for somebody as small as that to score points against an all-powerful grown-up. Even so, she was determined to have a go. Her father, after what had happened in front of the telly that evening, was first on her list.

The Hat
and the Superglue

The following morning, just before the father left for his beastly second-hand car garage, Matilda slipped into the cloakroom and got hold of the hat he wore each day to work. She had to stand on her toes and reach up as high as she could with a walking-stick in order to hook the hat off the peg, and even then she only just made it. The hat itself was one of those flat-topped pork-pie jobs with a jay's feather stuck in the hat-band and Mr Wormwood was very proud of it. He thought it gave him a rakish daring look, especially when he wore it at an angle with his loud checked jacket and green tie.

Matilda, holding the hat in one hand and a thin tube of Superglue in the other, proceeded to squeeze a line of glue very neatly all round the inside rim of the hat. Then she carefully hooked the hat back on to the peg with the walking-stick. She timed this operation very carefully, applying the glue just as her father was getting up from the breakfast table.

Mr Wormwood didn't notice anything when he put the hat on, but when he arrived at the garage he couldn't get it off. Superglue is very powerful stuff, so powerful it will take your skin off if you pull too hard. Mr Wormwood didn't want to be

scalped so he had to keep the hat on his head the whole day long, even when putting sawdust in gear-boxes and fiddling the mileages of cars with his electric drill. In an effort to save face, he adopted a casual attitude hoping that his staff would think that he actually *meant* to keep his hat on all day long just for the heck of it, like gangsters do in the films.

When he got home that evening he still couldn't get the hat off. "Don't be silly," his wife said. "Come here. I'll take it off for you."

She gave the hat a sharp yank. Mr Wormwood let out a yell that rattled the window-panes. "Ow-w-w!" he screamed. "Don't do that! Let go! You'll take half the skin off my forehead!"

Matilda, nestling in her usual chair, was watching this performance over the rim of her book with some interest.

"What's the matter, daddy?" she said. "Has your head suddenly swollen or something?"

The father glared at his daughter with deep suspicion, but said nothing. How could he? Mrs Wormwood said to him, "It *must* be Superglue. It couldn't be anything else. That'll teach you to go playing round with nasty stuff like that. I expect you were trying to stick another feather in your hat."

"I haven't touched the flaming stuff!" Mr Wormwood shouted. He turned and looked again at Matilda who looked back at him with large innocent brown eyes.

Mrs Wormwood said to him, "You should read the label on the tube before you start messing with dangerous products. Always follow the instructions on the label."

"What in heaven's name are you talking about, you stupid witch?" Mr Wormwood shouted, clutching the brim of his hat to stop anyone trying to pull it off again. "D'you think I'm so stupid I'd glue this thing to my head on purpose?"

Matilda said, "There's a boy down the road who got some Superglue on his finger without knowing it and then he put his finger to his nose."

Mr Wormwood jumped. "What happened to him?" he spluttered.

"The finger got stuck inside his nose," Matilda said, "and he had to go around like that for a week. People kept saying to him, 'Stop picking your nose,' and he couldn't do anything about it. He looked an awful fool."

"Serve him right," Mrs Wormwood said. "He shouldn't have put his finger up there in the first place. It's a nasty habit. If all children had Superglue put on their fingers they'd soon stop doing it."

Matilda said, "Grown-ups do it too, mummy. I saw you doing it yesterday in the kitchen."

"That's quite enough from you," Mrs Wormwood said, turning pink.

34

Mr Wormwood had to keep his hat on all through supper in front of the television. He looked ridiculous and he stayed very silent.

When he went up to bed he tried again to get the thing off, and so did his wife, but it wouldn't budge. "How am I going to have my shower?" he demanded.

"You'll just have to do without it, won't you," his wife told him. And later on, as she watched her skinny little husband skulking around the bedroom in his purple-striped pyjamas with a pork-pie hat on his head, she thought how stupid he looked. Hardly the kind of man a wife dreams about, she told herself.

Mr Wormwood discovered that the worst thing about having a permanent hat on his head was having to sleep in it. It was impossible to lie comfortably on the pillow. "Now do stop fussing around," his wife said to him after he had been tossing and turning for about an hour. "I expect it will be loose by the morning and then it'll slip off easily."

But it wasn't loose by the morning and it wouldn't slip off. So Mrs Wormwood took a pair of scissors and cut the thing off his head, bit by bit, first the top and then the brim. Where the inner band had stuck to the hair all around the sides and back, she had to chop the hair off right to the skin so that he finished up with a bald white ring round his head, like some sort of a monk. And in the front, where the band had stuck directly to the bare skin, there remained a whole lot of small patches of brown leathery stuff that no amount of washing would get off.

At breakfast Matilda said to him, "You *must* try to get those bits off your forehead, daddy. It looks as though you've got little brown insects crawling about all over you. People will think you've got lice."

"Be quiet!" the father snapped. "Just keep your nasty mouth shut, will you!"

All in all it was a most satisfactory exercise. But it was surely too much to hope that it had taught the father a permanent lesson.

The Ghost

There was comparative calm in the Wormwood household for about a week after the Superglue episode. The experience had clearly chastened Mr Wormwood and he seemed temporarily to have lost his taste for boasting and bullying.

Then suddenly he struck again. Perhaps he had had a bad day at the garage and had not sold enough crummy second-hand cars. There are many things that make a man irritable when he arrives home from work in the evening and a sensible wife will usually notice the storm-signals and will leave him alone until he simmers down.

When Mr Wormwood arrived back from the garage that evening his face was as dark as a thundercloud and somebody was clearly for the high-jump pretty soon. His wife recognised the signs immediately and made herself scarce. He then strode into the living-room. Matilda happened to be curled up in an arm-chair in the corner, totally absorbed in a book. Mr Wormwood switched on the television. The screen lit up. The programme blared. Mr Wormwood glared at Matilda. She hadn't moved. She had somehow trained herself by now to block her ears to the ghastly sound of the dreaded box. She kept right on reading, and for some reason this infuriated the father. Perhaps his anger was

intensified because he saw her getting pleasure from something that was beyond his reach.

"Don't you *ever* stop reading?" he snapped at her.

"Oh, hello daddy," she said pleasantly. "Did you have a good day?"

"What is this trash?" he said, snatching the book from her hands.

"It isn't trash, daddy, it's lovely. It's called *The Red Pony*. It's by John Steinbeck, an American writer. Why don't you try it? You'll love it."

"Filth," Mr Wormwood said. "If it's by an American it's certain to be filth. That's all they write about."

"No daddy, it's beautiful, honestly it is. It's about . . ."

"I don't want to know what it's about," Mr Wormwood barked. "I'm fed up with your reading anyway. Go and find yourself something useful to

do." With frightening suddenness he now began ripping the pages out of the book in handfuls and throwing them in the waste-paper basket.

Matilda froze in horror. The father kept going. There seemed little doubt that the man felt some kind of jealousy. How dare she, he seemed to be saying with each rip of a page, how dare she enjoy reading books when he couldn't? How dare she?

"That's a *library* book!" Matilda cried. "It doesn't belong to me! I have to return it to Mrs Phelps!"

"Then you'll have to buy another one, won't you?" the father said, still tearing out pages. "You'll have to save your pocket-money until there's enough in the kitty to buy a new one for your precious Mrs Phelps, won't you?" With that he dropped the now empty covers of the book into the basket and marched out of the room, leaving the telly blaring.

Most children in Matilda's place would have burst into floods of tears. She didn't do this. She sat there very still and white and thoughtful. She seemed to know that neither crying nor sulking ever got anyone anywhere. The only sensible thing to do when you are attacked is, as Napoleon once said, to counter-attack. Matilda's wonderfully subtle mind was already at work devising yet another suitable punishment for the poisonous parent. The plan that was now beginning to hatch in her mind depended, however, upon whether or not Fred's parrot was really as good a talker as Fred made out.

41

Fred was a friend of Matilda's. He was a small boy of six who lived just around the corner from her, and for days he had been going on about this great talking parrot his father had given him.

So the following afternoon, as soon as Mrs Wormwood had departed in her car for another session of bingo, Matilda set out for Fred's house to investigate. She knocked on his door and asked if he would be kind enough to show her the famous bird. Fred was delighted and led her up to his bedroom where a truly magnificent blue and yellow parrot sat in a tall cage.

"There it is," Fred said. "It's name is Chopper."

"Make it talk," Matilda said.

"You can't *make* it talk," Fred said. "You have to be patient. It'll talk when it feels like it."

They hung around, waiting. Suddenly the parrot said, "Hullo, hullo, hullo." It was exactly like a human voice. Matilda said, "That's amazing! What else can it say?"

"Rattle my bones!" the parrot said, giving a wonderful imitation of a spooky voice. "Rattle my bones!"

"He's always saying that," Fred told her .

"What else can he say?" Matilda asked.

"That's about it," Fred said. "But it is pretty marvellous don't you think?"

"It's fabulous," Matilda said. "Will you lend him to me just for one night?"

"No," Fred said. "Certainly not."

"I'll give you all my next week's pocket-money," Matilda said.

That was different. Fred thought about it for a few seconds. "All right, then," he said, "If you promise to return him tomorrow."

Matilda staggered back to her own empty house carrying the tall cage in both hands. There was a large fireplace in the dining-room and she now set about wedging the cage up the chimney and out of sight. This wasn't so easy, but she managed it in the end.

"Hullo, hullo, hullo!" the bird called down to her. "Hullo, hullo!"

"Shut up, you nut!" Matilda said, and she went out to wash the soot off her hands.

That evening while the mother, the father, the brother and Matilda were having supper as usual in the living-room in front of the television, a voice came loud and clear from the dining-room across the hall. "Hullo, hullo, hullo," it said.

"Harry!" cried the mother, turning white. "There's someone in the house! I heard a voice!"

"So did I!" the brother said. Matilda jumped up and switched off the telly. "Ssshh!" she said. "Listen!"

They all stopped eating and sat there very tense, listening.

"Hullo, hullo, hullo!" came the voice again.

"There it is!" cried the brother.

"It's burglars!" hissed the mother. "They're in the dining-room!"

"I think they are," the father said, sitting tight.

"Then go and catch them, Harry!" hissed the mother. "Go out and collar them red-handed!"

The father didn't move. He seemed in no hurry to dash off and be a hero. His face had turned grey.

"Get on with it!" hissed the mother. "They're probably after the silver!"

The husband wiped his lips nervously with his napkin. "Why don't we all go and look together?" he said.

"Come on, then," the brother said. "Come on, mum."

"They're definitely in the dining-room," Matilda whispered. "I'm sure they are."

The mother grabbed a poker from the fireplace. The father took a golf-club that was standing in the corner. The brother seized a table-lamp, ripping the plug out of its socket. Matilda took the knife she had been eating with, and all four of them crept towards the dining-room door, the father keeping well behind the others.

"Hullo, hullo, hullo," came the voice again.

"Come on!" Matilda cried and she burst into the room, brandishing her knife. "Stick 'em up!" she yelled. "We've caught you!" The others followed

her, waving their weapons. Then they stopped. They stared around the room. There was no one there.

"There's no one here," the father said, greatly relieved.

"I heard him, Harry!" the mother shrieked, still quaking. "I distinctly heard his voice! So did you!"

"I'm certain I heard him!" Matilda cried. "He's in here somewhere!" She began searching behind the sofa and behind the curtains.

Then came the voice once again, soft and spooky this time, "Rattle my bones," it said. "Rattle my bones."

They all jumped, including Matilda who was a pretty good actress. They stared round the room. There was still no one there.

"It's a ghost," Matilda said.

"Heaven help us!" cried the mother, clutching her husband round the neck.

"I know it's a ghost!" Matilda said. "I've heard it here before! This room is haunted! I thought you knew that."

"Save us!" the mother screamed, almost throttling her husband.

"I'm getting out of here," the father said, greyer than ever now. They all fled, slamming the door behind them.

The next afternoon, Matilda managed to get a rather sooty and grumpy parrot down from the chimney and out of the house without being seen. She carried it through the back-door and ran with it all the way to Fred's house.

"Did it behave itself?" Fred asked her.

"We had a lovely time with it," Matilda said. "My parents adored it."

Arithmetic

Matilda longed for her parents to be good and loving and understanding and honourable and intelligent. The fact that they were none of these things was something she had to put up with. It was not easy to do so. But the new game she had invented of punishing one or both of them each time they were beastly to her made her life more or less bearable.

Being very small and very young, the only power Matilda had over anyone in her family was brain-power. For sheer cleverness she could run rings around them all. But the fact remained that any five-year-old girl in any family was always obliged to do as she was told, however asinine the orders might be. Thus she was always forced to eat her evening meals out of TV-dinner-trays in front of the dreaded box. She always had to stay alone on weekday afternoons, and whenever she was told to shut up, she had to shut up.

Her safety-valve, the thing that prevented her from going round the bend, was the fun of devising and dishing out these splendid punishments, and the lovely thing was that they seemed to work, at any rate for short periods. The father in particular became less cocky and unbearable for several days after receiving a dose of Matilda's magic medicine.

The parrot-in-the-chimney affair quite definitely

49

cooled both parents down a lot and for over a week they were comparatively civil to their small daughter. But alas, this couldn't last. The next flare-up came one evening in the sitting-room. Mr Wormwood had just returned from work. Matilda and her brother were sitting quietly on the sofa waiting for their mother to bring in the TV dinners on a tray. The television had not yet been switched on.

In came Mr Wormwood in a loud check suit and a yellow tie. The appalling broad orange-and-green check of the jacket and trousers almost blinded the onlooker. He looked like a low-grade bookmaker dressed up for his daughter's wedding, and he was clearly very pleased with himself this evening. He sat down in an armchair and rubbed his hands together and addressed his son in a loud voice. "Well, my boy," he said, "your father's had a most successful day. He is a lot richer tonight than he was this morning. He has sold no less than five cars, each one at a tidy profit. Sawdust in the gear-boxes, the electric-drill on the speedometer cables, a splash of paint here and there and a few other clever little tricks and the idiots were all falling over themselves to buy."

He fished a bit of paper from his pocket and studied it. "Listen boy," he said, addressing the son and ignoring Matilda, "seeing as you'll be going into this business with me one day, you've got to know how to add up the profits you make at the end of each day. Go and get yourself a pad and a pencil and let's see how clever you are."

The son obediently left the room and returned with the writing materials.

"Write down these figures," the father said, reading from his bit of paper. "Car number one was bought by me for two hundred and seventy-eight pounds and sold for one thousand four hundred and twenty-five. Got that?"

The ten-year-old boy wrote the two separate amounts down slowly and carefully.

"Car number two", the father went on, "cost me one hundred and eighteen pounds and sold for seven hundred and sixty. Got it?"

"Yes, dad," the son said. "I've got that."

"Car number three cost one hundred and eleven pounds and sold for nine hundred and ninety-nine pounds and fifty pence."

"Say that again," the son said. "How much did it sell for?"

"Nine hundred and ninety-nine pounds and fifty pence," the father said. "And that, by the way, is another of my nifty little tricks to diddle the customer. Never ask for a big round figure. Always go just below it. Never say one thousand pounds. Always say nine hundred and ninety-nine fifty. It sounds much less but it isn't. Clever, isn't it?"

"Very," the son said. "You're brilliant, dad."

"Car number four cost eighty-six pounds – a real wreck that was – and sold for six hundred and ninety-nine pounds fifty."

"Not too fast," the son said, writing the numbers down. "Right. I've got it."

"Car number five cost six hundred and thirty-seven pounds and sold for sixteen hundred and forty-nine fifty. You got all those figures written down, son?"

"Yes, daddy," the boy said, crouching over his pad and carefully writing.

"Very well," the father said. "Now work out the profit I made on each of the five cars and add up the total. Then you'll be able to tell me how much money your rather brilliant father made altogether today."

"That's a lot of sums," the boy said.

"Of course it's a lot of sums," the father answered. "But when you're in big business like I am, you've got to be hot stuff at arithmetic. I've practically got a computer inside my head. It took me less than ten minutes to work the whole thing out."

"You mean you did it in your head, dad?" the son asked, goggling.

"Well, not exactly," the father said. "Nobody could do that. But it didn't take me long. When you're finished, tell me what you think my profit was for the day. I've got the final total written down here and I'll tell you if you're right."

Matilda said quietly, "Dad, you made exactly four thousand three hundred and three pounds and fifty pence altogether."

"Don't butt in," the father said. "Your brother and I are busy with high finance."

"But dad . . . "

"Shut up," the father said. "Stop guessing and trying to be clever."

"Look at your answer, dad," Matilda said gently. "If you've done it right it ought to be four thousand three hundred and three pounds and fifty pence. Is that what you've got, dad?"

The father glanced down at the paper in his hand. He seemed to stiffen. He became very quiet. There was a silence. Then he said, "Say that again."

"Four thousand three hundred and three pounds fifty," Matilda said.

There was another silence. The father's face was beginning to go dark red.

"I'm sure it's right," Matilda said.

"You . . . you little cheat!" the father suddenly shouted, pointing at her with his finger. "You looked at my bit of paper! You read it off from what I've got written here!"

"Daddy, I'm the other side of the room," Matilda said. "How could I possibly see it?"

"Don't give me that rubbish!" the father shouted. "Of course you looked! You must have looked! No one in the world could give the right answer just like that, especially a girl! You're a little cheat, madam, that's what you are! A cheat and a liar!"

At that point, the mother came in carrying a large tray on which were the four suppers. This time it was fish and chips which Mrs Wormwood had picked up in the fish and chip shop on her way home from bingo. It seemed that bingo afternoons left her so exhausted both physically and emotionally that she never had enough energy left to cook an evening meal. So if it wasn't TV dinners it had to be fish and chips. "What are you looking so red in the face about, Harry?" she said as she put the tray down on the coffee-table.

"Your daughter's a cheat and a liar," the father said, taking his plate of fish and placing it on his knees. "Turn the telly on and let's not have any more talk."

The Platinum-Blond Man

There was no doubt in Matilda's mind that this latest display of foulness by her father deserved severe punishment, and as she sat eating her awful fried fish and fried chips and ignoring the television, her brain went to work on various possibilities. By the time she went up to bed her mind was made up.

The next morning she got up early and went into the bathroom and locked the door. As we already know, Mrs Wormwood's hair was dyed a brilliant platinum blonde, very much the same glistening silvery colour as a female tightrope-walker's tights in a circus. The big dyeing job was done twice a year at the hairdresser's, but every month or so in between, Mrs Wormwood used to freshen it up by giving it a rinse in the washbasin with something called PLATINUM BLONDE HAIR-DYE EXTRA STRONG. This also served to dye the nasty brown hairs that kept growing from the roots underneath. The bottle of PLATINUM BLONDE HAIR-DYE EXTRA STRONG was kept in the cupboard in the bathroom, and underneath the title on the label were written the words *Caution, this is peroxide. Keep away from children*. Matilda had read it many times with fascination.

Matilda's father had a fine crop of black hair

which he parted in the middle and of which he was exceedingly proud. "Good strong hair," he was fond of saying, "means there's a good strong brain underneath."

"Like Shakespeare," Matilda had once said to him.

"Like who?"

"Shakespeare, daddy."

"Was he brainy?"

"Very, daddy."

"He had masses of hair, did he?"

"He was bald, daddy."

To which the father had snapped, "If you can't talk sense then shut up."

Anyway, Mr Wormwood kept his hair looking bright and strong, or so he thought, by rubbing into it every morning large quantities of a lotion called OIL OF VIOLETS HAIR TONIC. A bottle of this smelly purple mixture always stood on the shelf above the sink in the bathroom alongside all the toothbrushes, and a very vigorous scalp massage with OIL OF VIOLETS took place daily after shaving was completed. This hair and scalp massage was always accompanied by loud masculine grunts and heavy

breathing and gasps of "Ahhh, that's better! That's
the stuff! Rub it right into the roots!" which could
be clearly heard by Matilda in her bedroom across
the corridor.

Now, in the early morning privacy of the bathroom, Matilda unscrewed the cap of her father's
OIL OF VIOLETS and tipped three-quarters of the
contents down the drain. Then she filled the bottle
up with her mother's PLATINUM BLONDE HAIR-DYE
EXTRA STRONG. She carefully left enough of her
father's original hair tonic in the bottle so that
when she gave it a good shake the whole thing still
looked reasonably purple. She then replaced the
bottle on the shelf above the sink, taking care to
put her mother's bottle back in the cupboard. So
far so good.

At breakfast time Matilda sat quietly at the
dining-room table eating her cornflakes. Her
brother sat opposite her with his back to the door
devouring hunks of bread smothered with a mixture of peanut-butter and strawberry jam. The
mother was just out of sight around the corner
in the kitchen making Mr Wormwood's breakfast
which always had to be two fried eggs on fried
bread with three pork sausages and three strips of
bacon and some fried tomatoes.

At this point Mr Wormwood came noisily into
the room. He was incapable of entering any room
quietly, especially at breakfast time. He always
had to make his appearance felt immediately by
creating a lot of noise and clatter. One could almost
hear him saying, "It's me! Here I come, the great

man himself, the master of the house, the wage-earner, the one who makes it possible for all the rest of you to live so well! Notice me and pay your respects!"

On this occasion he strode in and slapped his son on the back and shouted, "Well my boy, your father feels he's in for another great money-making day today at the garage! I've got a few little beauties I'm going to flog to the idiots this morning. Where's my breakfast?"

"It's coming, treasure," Mrs Wormwood called from the kitchen.

Matilda kept her face bent low over her corn-flakes. She didn't dare look up. In the first place she wasn't at all sure what she was going to see. And secondly, if she did see what she thought she was going to see, she wouldn't trust herself to keep a straight face. The son was looking directly ahead out of the window stuffing himself with bread and peanut-butter and strawberry jam.

The father was just moving round to sit at the head of the table when the mother came sweeping out from the kitchen carrying a huge plate piled high with eggs and sausages and bacon and tom-atoes. She looked up. She caught sight of her hus-band. She stopped dead. Then she let out a scream that seemed to lift her right up into the air and she dropped the plate with a crash and a splash on to the floor. Everyone jumped, including Mr Wormwood.

"What the heck's the matter with you, woman?" he shouted. "Look at the mess you've made on the carpet!"

"Your *hair*!" the mother was shrieking, pointing a quivering finger at her husband. "Look at your *hair*! What've you done to your *hair*?"

"What's wrong with my hair for heaven's sake?" he said.

"Oh my gawd dad, what've you done to your hair?" the son shouted.

A splendid noisy scene was building up nicely in the breakfast room.

Matilda said nothing. She simply sat there admiring the wonderful effect of her own handiwork. Mr Wormwood's fine crop of black hair was now a dirty silver, the colour this time of a tightrope-walker's tights that had not been washed for the entire circus season.

"You've . . . you've . . . you've *dyed* it!" shrieked the mother. "Why did you do it, you fool! It looks absolutely frightful! It looks horrendous! You look like a freak!"

"What the blazes are you all talking about?" the father yelled, putting both hands to his hair. "I most certainly have not dyed it! What d'you mean I've dyed it? What's happened to it? Or is this some sort of a stupid joke?" His face was turning pale green, the colour of sour apples.

"You *must* have dyed it, dad," the son said. "It's the same colour as mum's only much dirtier looking."

"Of course he's dyed it!" the mother cried. "It can't change colour all by itself! What on earth were you trying to do, make yourself look handsome or something? You look like someone's grandmother gone wrong!"

"Get me a mirror!" the father yelled. "Don't just stand there shrieking at me! Get me a mirror!"

The mother's handbag lay on a chair at the other end of the table. She opened the bag and got out a powder compact that had a small round mirror on the inside of the lid. She opened the compact and handed it to her husband. He grabbed it and held it before his face and in doing so spilled most of

the powder all over the front of his fancy tweed
jacket.

"Be *careful*!" shrieked the mother. "Now look
what you've done! That's my best Elizabeth Arden
face powder!"

"Oh my gawd!" yelled the father, staring into
the little mirror. "What's happened to me! I look
terrible! I look just like *you* gone wrong! I can't go
down to the garage and sell cars like this! How did
it happen?" He stared round the room, first at the
mother, then at the son, then at Matilda. "How
could it have happened?" he yelled.

"I imagine, daddy," Matilda said quietly, "that
you weren't looking very hard and you simply took
mummy's bottle of hair stuff off the shelf instead
of your own."

"*Of course* that's what happened!" the mother cried. "Well really Harry, how stupid can you get? Why didn't you read the label before you started splashing the stuff all over you! Mine's *terribly* strong. I'm only meant to use one tablespoon of it in a whole basin of water and you've gone and put it all over your head neat! It'll probably take all your hair off in the end! Is your scalp beginning to burn, dear?"

"You mean I'm going to lose all my hair?" the husband yelled.

"I think you will," the mother said. "Peroxide is a very powerful chemical. It's what they put down the lavatory to disinfect the pan only they give it another name."

"What are you saying!" the husband cried. "I'm not a lavatory pan! I don't want to be disinfected!"

"Even diluted like I use it," the mother told him, "it makes a good deal of *my* hair fall out, so goodness knows what's going to happen to you. I'm surprised it didn't take the whole of the top of your head off!"

"What shall I do?" wailed the father. "Tell me quick what to do before it starts falling out!"

Matilda said, "I'd give it a good wash, dad, if I were you, with soap and water. But you'll have to hurry."

"Will that change the colour back?" the father asked anxiously.

"Of course it won't, you twit," the mother said.

"Then what do I do? I can't go around looking like this for ever?"

64

"You'll have to have it dyed black," the mother said. "But wash it first or there won't be any there to dye."

"Right!" the father shouted, springing into action. "Get me an appointment with your hairdresser this instant for a hair-dyeing job! Tell them it's an emergency! They've got to boot someone else off their list! I'm going upstairs to wash it now!" With that the man dashed out of the room and Mrs Wormwood, sighing deeply, went to the telephone to call the beauty parlour.

"He does do some pretty silly things now and again, doesn't he, mummy?" Matilda said.

The mother, dialling the number on the phone, said, "I'm afraid men are not always quite as clever as they think they are. You will learn that when you get a bit older, my girl."

Miss Honey

Matilda was a little late in starting school. Most children begin Primary School at five or even just before, but Matilda's parents, who weren't very concerned one way or the other about their daughter's education, had forgotten to make the proper arrangements in advance. She was five and a half when she entered school for the first time.

The village school for younger children was a bleak brick building called Crunchem Hall Primary School. It had about two hundred and fifty pupils aged from five to just under twelve years old. The head teacher, the boss, the supreme commander of this establishment was a formidable middle-aged lady whose name was Miss Trunchbull.

Naturally Matilda was put in the bottom class, where there were eighteen other small boys and girls about the same age as her. Their teacher was called Miss Honey, and she could not have been more than twenty-three or twenty-four. She had a lovely pale oval madonna face with blue eyes and her hair was light-brown. Her body was so slim and fragile one got the feeling that if she fell over she would smash into a thousand pieces, like a porcelain figure.

Miss Jennifer Honey was a mild and quiet person who never raised her voice and was seldom seen to smile, but there is no doubt she possessed that rare gift for being adored by every small child under her care. She seemed to understand totally the bewilderment and fear that so often overwhelms young children who for the first time in their lives are herded into a classroom and told to obey orders. Some curious warmth that was almost tangible shone out of Miss Honey's face when she spoke to a confused and homesick newcomer to the class.

Miss Trunchbull, the Headmistress, was something else altogether. She was a gigantic holy terror, a fierce tyrannical monster who frightened the life out of the pupils and teachers alike. There was an aura of menace about her even at a distance, and when she came up close you could almost feel the dangerous heat radiating from her as from a red-hot rod of metal. When she marched – Miss Trunchbull never walked, she always marched like a stormtrooper with long strides and arms aswinging – when she marched along a corridor you could actually hear her snorting as she went, and if a group of children happened to be in her path, she ploughed right on through them like a tank, with small people bouncing off her to left and right. Thank goodness we don't meet many people like her in this world, although they do exist and all of us are likely to come across at least one of them in a lifetime. If you ever do, you should behave as you would if you met an enraged rhinoceros out in the bush – climb up the nearest tree and stay there until it has gone away. This woman, in all her eccentricities and in her appearance, is almost im-

possible to describe, but I shall make some attempt to do so a little later on. Let us leave her for the moment and go back to Matilda and her first day in Miss Honey's class.

After the usual business of going through all the names of the children, Miss Honey handed out a brand-new exercise-book to each pupil.

"You have all brought your own pencils, I hope," she said.

"Yes, Miss Honey," they chanted.

"Good. Now this is the very first day of school for each one of you. It is the beginning of at least eleven long years of schooling that all of you are going to have to go through. And six of those years will be spent right here at Crunchem Hall where, as you know, your Headmistress is Miss Trunchbull. Let me for your own good tell you something about Miss Trunchbull. She insists upon strict discipline throughout the school, and if you take my advice you will do your very best to behave yourselves in her presence. Never argue with her. Never answer her back. Always do as she says. If you get on the wrong side of Miss Trunchbull she can liquidise you like a carrot in a kitchen blender. It's nothing to laugh about, Lavender. Take that grin off your face. All of you will be wise to remember that Miss Trunchbull deals very very severely with anyone who gets out of line in this school. Have you got the message?"

"Yes, Miss Honey," chirruped eighteen eager little voices.

"I myself", Miss Honey went on, "want to help you to learn as much as possible while you are in this class. That is because I know it will make things easier for you later on. For example, by the end of this week I shall expect every one of you to know the two-times table by heart. And in a year's time I hope you will know all the multiplication tables up to twelve. It will help you enormously if you do. Now then, do any of you happen to have learnt the two-times table already?"

Matilda put up her hand. She was the only one.

Miss Honey looked carefully at the tiny girl with dark hair and a round serious face sitting in the second row. "Wonderful," she said. "Please stand up and recite as much of it as you can."

Matilda stood up and began to say the two-times table. When she got to twice twelve is twenty-four she didn't stop. She went right on with twice thirteen is twenty-six, twice fourteen is twenty-eight, twice fifteen is thirty, twice sixteen is . . . "

"Stop!" Miss Honey said. She had been listening slightly spellbound to this smooth recital, and now she said, "How far can you go?"

"How far?" Matilda said. "Well, I don't really

know, Miss Honey. For quite a long way, I think."

Miss Honey took a few moments to let this curious statement sink in. "You mean", she said, "that you could tell me what two times twenty-eight is?"

"Yes, Miss Honey."

"What is it?"

"Fifty-six, Miss Honey."

"What about something much harder, like two times four hundred and eighty-seven? Could you tell me that?"

"I think so, yes," Matilda said.

"Are you sure?"

"Why yes, Miss Honey, I'm fairly sure."

"What is it then, two times four hundred and eighty-seven?"

"Nine hundred and seventy-four," Matilda said immediately. She spoke quietly and politely and without any sign of showing off.

Miss Honey gazed at Matilda with absolute amazement, but when next she spoke she kept her voice level. "That is really splendid," she said. "But of course multiplying by two is a lot easier than some of the bigger numbers. What about the other multiplication tables? Do you know any of those?"

"I think so, Miss Honey. I think I do."

"Which ones, Matilda? How far have you got?"

"I . . . I don't quite know," Matilda said. "I don't know what you mean."

"What I mean is do you for instance know the three-times table?"

"Yes, Miss Honey."

"And the four-times?"

"Yes, Miss Honey."

"Well, how many *do* you know, Matilda? Do you know all the way up to the twelve-times table?"

"Yes, Miss Honey."

"What are twelve sevens?"

"Eighty-four," Matilda said.

Miss Honey paused and leaned back in her chair behind the plain table that stood in the middle of the floor in front of the class. She was considerably shaken by this exchange but took care not to show it. She had never come across a five-year-old before, or indeed a ten-year-old, who could multiply with such facility.

"I hope the rest of you are listening to this," she said to the class. "Matilda is a very lucky girl. She has wonderful parents who have already taught her to multiply lots of numbers. Was it your mother, Matilda, who taught you?"

"No, Miss Honey, it wasn't."

"You must have a great father then. He must be a brilliant teacher."

"No, Miss Honey," Matilda said quietly. "My father did not teach me."

"You mean you taught yourself?"

"I don't quite know," Matilda said truthfully. "It's just that I don't find it very difficult to multiply one number by another."

Miss Honey took a deep breath and let it out slowly. She looked again at the small girl with bright eyes standing beside her desk so sensible and solemn. "You say you don't find it difficult to multiply one number by another," Miss Honey said. "Could you try to explain that a little bit."

73

"Oh dear," Matilda said. "I'm not really sure."

Miss Honey waited. The class was silent, all listening.

"For instance," Miss Honey said, "if I asked you to multiply fourteen by nineteen . . . No, that's too difficult . . . "

"It's two hundred and sixty-six," Matilda said softly.

Miss Honey stared at her. Then she picked up a pencil and quickly worked out the sum on a piece of paper. "What did you say it was?" she said, looking up.

"Two hundred and sixty-six," Matilda said.

Miss Honey put down her pencil and removed her spectacles and began to polish the lenses with a piece of tissue. The class remained quiet, watching her and waiting for what was coming next. Matilda was still standing up beside her desk.

"Now tell me, Matilda," Miss Honey said, still polishing, "try to tell me exactly what goes on inside your head when you get a multiplication like that to do. You obviously have to work it out in some way, but you seem able to arrive at the answer almost instantly. Take the one you've just done, fourteen multiplied by nineteen."

"I . . . I . . . I simply put the fourteen down in my head and multiply it by nineteen," Matilda said. "I'm afraid I don't know how else to explain it. I've always said to myself that if a little pocket calculator can do it why shouldn't I?"

"Why not indeed," Miss Honey said. "The human brain is an amazing thing."

74

"I think it's a lot better than a lump of metal,"
Matilda said. "That's all a calculator is."

"How right you are," Miss Honey said. "Pocket
calculators are not allowed in this school anyway."
Miss Honey was feeling quite quivery. There was
no doubt in her mind that she had met a truly
extraordinary mathematical brain, and words like
child-genius and prodigy went flitting through her
head. She knew that these sort of wonders do pop
up in the world from time to time, but only once
or twice in a hundred years. After all, Mozart was
only five when he started composing for the piano
and look what happened to him.

"It's not fair," Lavender said. "How can she do
it and we can't?"

"Don't worry, Lavender, you'll soon catch up," Miss Honey said, lying through her teeth.

At this point Miss Honey could not resist the temptation of exploring still further the mind of this astonishing child. She knew that she ought to be paying some attention to the rest of the class but she was altogether too excited to let the matter rest.

"Well," she said, pretending to address the whole class, "let us leave sums for the moment and see if any of you have begun to learn to spell. Hands up anyone who can spell cat."

Three hands went up. They belonged to Lavender, a small boy called Nigel and to Matilda.

"Spell cat, Nigel."

Nigel spelled it.

Miss Honey now decided to ask a question that normally she would not have dreamed of asking the class on its first day. "I wonder", she said, "whether any of you three who know how to spell cat have learned how to read a whole group of words when they are strung together in a sentence?"

"I have," Nigel said.

"So have I," Lavender said.

Miss Honey went to the blackboard and wrote with her white chalk the sentence, *I have already begun to learn how to read long sentences*. She had purposely made it difficult and she knew that there were precious few five-year-olds around who would be able to manage it.

"Can you tell me what that says, Nigel?" she asked.

"That's too hard," Nigel said.

"Lavender?"

"The first word is I," Lavender said.

"Can any of you read the whole sentence?" Miss Honey asked, waiting for the "yes" that she felt certain was going to come from Matilda.

"Yes," Matilda said.

"Go ahead," Miss Honey said.

Matilda read the sentence without any hesitation at all.

"That really is very good indeed," Miss Honey said, making the understatement of her life. "How much *can* you read, Matilda?"

"I think I can read most things, Miss Honey," Matilda said, "although I'm afraid I can't always understand the meanings."

Miss Honey got to her feet and walked smartly out of the room, but was back in thirty seconds carrying a thick book. She opened it at random and placed it on Matilda's desk. "This is a book of humorous poetry," she said. "See if you can read that one aloud."

Smoothly, without a pause and at a nice speed, Matilda began to read:

"An epicure dining at Crewe
Found a rather large mouse in his stew.
Cried the waiter, "Don't shout
And wave it about
Or the rest will be wanting one too."

Several children saw the funny side of the rhyme

77

and laughed. Miss Honey said, "Do you know what an epicure is, Matilda?"

"It is someone who is dainty with his eating," Matilda said.

"That is correct," Miss Honey said. "And do you happen to know what that particular type of poetry is called?"

"It's called a limerick," Matilda said. "That's a lovely one. It's so funny."

"It's a famous one," Miss Honey said, picking up the book and returning to her table in front of the class. "A witty limerick is very hard to write," she added. "They look easy but they most certainly are not."

"I know," Matilda said. "I've tried quite a few times but mine are never any good."

"You have, have you?" Miss Honey said, more startled than ever. "Well Matilda, I would very much like to hear one of these limericks you say you have written. Could you try to remember one for us?"

"Well," Matilda said, hesitating. "I've actually been trying to make up one about you, Miss Honey, while we've been sitting here."

"About *me!*" Miss Honey cried. "Well, we've certainly got to hear that one, haven't we?"

"I don't think I want to say it, Miss Honey."

"Please tell it," Miss Honey said. "I promise I won't mind."

"I think you will, Miss Honey, because I have to use your first name to make things rhyme and that's why I don't want to say it."

"How do you know my first name?" Miss Honey asked.

"I heard another teacher calling you by it just before we came in," Matilda said. "She called you Jenny."

"I insist upon hearing this limerick," Miss Honey said, smiling one of her rare smiles. "Stand up and recite it."

Reluctantly Matilda stood up and very slowly, very nervously, she recited her limerick:

"The thing we all ask about Jenny
Is, 'Surely there cannot be many
Young girls in the place
With so lovely a face?'
The answer to that is, '*Not any!*'"

The whole of Miss Honey's pale and pleasant face blushed a brilliant scarlet. Then once again she smiled. It was a much broader one this time, a smile of pure pleasure.

79

"Why, thank you, Matilda," she said, still smiling. "Although it is not true, it is really a very good limerick. Oh dear, oh dear, I must try to remember that one."

From the third row of desks, Lavender said, "It's good. I like it."

"It's true as well," a small boy called Rupert said.

"Of course it's true," Nigel said.

Already the whole class had begun to warm towards Miss Honey, although as yet she had hardly taken any notice of any of them except Matilda.

"Who taught you to read, Matilda?" Miss Honey asked.

"I just sort of taught myself, Miss Honey."

"And have you read any books all by yourself, any children's books, I mean?"

"I've read all the ones that are in the public library in the High Street, Miss Honey."

"And did you like them?"

"I liked some of them very much indeed," Matilda said, "but I thought others were fairly dull."

"Tell me one that you liked."

"I liked *The Lion, the Witch and the Wardrobe*," Matilda said. "I think Mr C. S. Lewis is a very good writer. But he has one failing. There are no funny bits in his books."

"You are right there," Miss Honey said.

"There aren't many funny bits in Mr Tolkien either," Matilda said.

"Do you think that all children's books ought to have funny bits in them?" Miss Honey asked.

"I do," Matilda said. "Children are not so serious as grown-ups and they love to laugh."

Miss Honey was astounded by the wisdom of this tiny girl. She said, "And what are you going to do now that you've read all the children's books?"

"I am reading other books," Matilda said. "I borrow them from the library. Mrs Phelps is very kind to me. She helps me to choose them."

Miss Honey was leaning far forward over her work-table and gazing in wonder at the child. She had completely forgotten now about the rest of the class. "What other books?" she murmured.

"I am very fond of Charles Dickens," Matilda said. "He makes me laugh a lot. Especially Mr Pickwick."

At that moment the bell in the corridor sounded for the end of class.

The Trunchbull

In the interval, Miss Honey left the classroom and headed straight for the Headmistress's study. She felt wildly excited. She had just met a small girl who possessed, or so it seemed to her, quite extraordinary qualities of brilliance. There had not been time yet to find out exactly how brilliant the child was, but Miss Honey had learned enough to realise that something had to be done about it as soon as possible. It would be ridiculous to leave a child like that stuck in the bottom form.

Normally Miss Honey was terrified of the Headmistress and kept well away from her, but at this moment she felt ready to take on anybody. She knocked on the door of the dreaded private study. "Enter!" boomed the deep and dangerous voice of Miss Trunchbull. Miss Honey went in.

Now most head teachers are chosen because they possess a number of fine qualities. They understand children and they have the children's best interests at heart. They are sympathetic. They are fair and they are deeply interested in education. Miss Trunchbull possessed none of these qualities and how she ever got her present job was a mystery.

She was above all a most formidable female. She had once been a famous athlete, and even now the muscles were still clearly in evidence. You could see them in the bull-neck, in the big shoulders, in the thick arms, in the sinewy wrists and in the powerful legs. Looking at her, you got the feeling that this was someone who could bend iron bars and tear telephone directories in half. Her face, I'm afraid, was neither a thing of beauty nor a joy for ever. She had an obstinate chin, a cruel mouth and small arrogant eyes. And as for her clothes . . . they were, to say the least, extremely odd. She always had on a brown cotton smock which was pinched in around the waist with a wide leather belt. The belt was fastened in front with an enormous silver buckle. The massive thighs which emerged from out of the smock were encased in a pair of extraordinary breeches, bottle-green in colour and made of coarse twill. These breeches reached to just below the knees and from there on down she sported green stockings with turn-up tops, which displayed her calf muscles to perfection. On her feet she wore flat-heeled brown brogues with leather flaps. She looked, in short, more like a rather eccentric and bloodthirsty follower of the stag-hounds than the headmistress of a nice school for children.

When Miss Honey entered the study, Miss Trunchbull was standing beside her huge desk with a look of scowling impatience on her face. "Yes, Miss Honey," she said. "What is it you want? You're looking very flushed and flustered this morning. What's the matter with you? Have those little stinkers been flicking spitballs at you?"

"No, Headmistress. Nothing like that."

"Well, what is it then? Get on with it. I'm a busy

woman." As she spoke, she reached out and poured herself a glass of water from a jug that was always on her desk.

"There is a little girl in my class called Matilda Wormwood . . ." Miss Honey began.

"That's the daughter of the man who owns Wormwood Motors in the village," Miss Trunchbull barked. She hardly ever spoke in a normal voice. She either barked or shouted. "An excellent person, Wormwood," she went on. "I was in there only yesterday. He sold me a car. Almost new. Only done ten thousand miles. Previous owner was an old lady who took it out once a year at the most. A terrific bargain. Yes, I liked Wormwood. A real pillar of our society. He told me the daughter was a bad lot though. He said to watch her. He said if anything bad ever happened in the school, it was certain to be his daughter who did it. I haven't met the little brat yet, but she'll know about it when I do. Her father said she's a real wart."

"Oh no, Headmistress, that can't be right!" Miss Honey cried.

"Oh yes, Miss Honey, it darn well is right! In fact, now I come to think of it, I'll bet it was she who put that stink-bomb under my desk here first thing this morning. The place stank like a sewer! Of course it was her! I shall have her for that, you see if I don't! What's she look like? Nasty little worm, I'll be bound. I have discovered, Miss Honey, during my long career as a teacher that a bad girl is a far more dangerous creature than a bad boy. What's more, they're much harder to squash.

Squashing a bad girl is like trying to squash a bluebottle. You bang down on it and the darn thing isn't there. Nasty dirty things, little girls are. Glad I never was one."

"Oh, but you must have been a little girl once, Headmistress. Surely you were."

"Not for long anyway," Miss Trunchbull barked, grinning. "I became a woman very quickly."

She's completely off her rocker, Miss Honey told herself. She's barmy as a bedbug. Miss Honey stood resolutely before the Headmistress. For once she was not going to be browbeaten. "I must tell you, Headmistress," she said, "that you are completely mistaken about Matilda putting a stink-bomb under your desk."

"I am never mistaken, Miss Honey!"

"But Headmistress, the child only arrived in school this morning and came straight to the classroom . . . "

"Don't argue with me, for heaven's sake, woman! This little brute Matilda or whatever her name is has stink-bombed my study! There's no doubt about it! Thank you for suggesting it."

"But I didn't suggest it, Headmistress."

"Of course you did! Now what is it you want, Miss Honey? Why are you wasting my time?"

"I came to you to talk about Matilda, Headmistress. I have extraordinary things to report about the child. May I please tell you what happened in class just now?"

"I suppose she set fire to your skirt and scorched your knickers!" Miss Trunchbull snorted.

"No, no!" Miss Honey cried out. "Matilda is a genius."

At the mention of this word, Miss Trunchbull's face turned purple and her whole body seemed to swell up like a bullfrog's. "A *genius*!" she shouted. "What piffle is this you are talking, madam? You must be out of your mind! I have her father's word for it that the child is a gangster!"

"Her father is wrong, Headmistress."

"Don't be a twerp, Miss Honey! You have met the little beast for only half an hour and her father has known her all her life!"

But Miss Honey was determined to have her say and she now began to describe some of the amazing things Matilda had done with arithmetic.

"So she's learnt a few tables by heart, has she?" Miss Trunchbull barked. "My dear woman, that doesn't make her a genius! It makes her a parrot!"

"But Headmistress she can *read*."

"So can I," Miss Trunchbull snapped.

"It is my opinion", Miss Honey said, "that Matilda should be taken out of my form and placed immediately in the top form with the eleven-year-olds."

"Ha!" snorted Miss Trunchbull. "So you want to get rid of her, do you? So you can't handle her? So now you want to unload her on to the wretched Miss Plimsoll in the top form where she will cause even more chaos?"

"No, no!" cried Miss Honey. "That is not my reason at all!"

"Oh, yes it is!" shouted Miss Trunchbull. "I can see right through your little plot, madam! And my answer is no! Matilda stays where she is and it is up to you to see that she behaves herself."

"But Headmistress, please . . . "

"Not another word!" shouted Miss Trunchbull. "And in any case, I have a rule in this school that all children remain in their own age groups

88

regardless of ability. Great Scott, I'm not having a little five-year-old brigand sitting with the senior girls and boys in the top form. Whoever heard of such a thing!"

Miss Honey stood there helpless before this great red-necked giant. There was a lot more she would like to have said but she knew it was useless. She said softly, "Very well, then. It's up to you, Headmistress."

"You're darn right it's up to me!" Miss Trunchbull bellowed. "And don't forget, madam, that we are dealing here with a little viper who put a stink-bomb under my desk . . . "

"She did *not* do that, Headmistress!"

"Of course she did it," Miss Trunchbull boomed. "And I'll tell you what. I wish to heavens I was still allowed to use the birch and belt as I did in the good old days! I'd have roasted Matilda's bottom for her so she couldn't sit down for a month!"

Miss Honey turned and walked out of the study feeling depressed but by no means defeated. I am going to do something about this child, she told herself. I don't know what it will be, but I shall find a way to help her in the end.

The Parents

When Miss Honey emerged from the Head-mistress's study, most of the children were outside in the playground. Her first move was to go round to the various teachers who taught the senior class and borrow from them a number of text-books, books on algebra, geometry, French, English Literature and the like. Then she sought out Matilda and called her into the classroom.

"There is no point", she said, "in you sitting in class doing nothing while I am teaching the rest of the form the two-times table and how to spell cat and rat and mouse. So during each lesson I shall give you one of these text-books to study. At the end of the lesson you can come up to me with your questions if you have any and I shall try to help you. How does that sound?"

"Thank you, Miss Honey," Matilda said. "That sounds fine."

"I am sure," Miss Honey said, "that we'll be able to get you moved into a much higher form later on, but for the moment the Headmistress wishes you to stay where you are."

"Very well, Miss Honey," Matilda said. "Thank you so much for getting those books for me."

What a nice child she is, Miss Honey thought. I don't care what her father said about her, she seems very quiet and gentle to me. And not a bit stuck up in spite of her brilliance. In fact she hardly seems aware of it.

So when the class reassembled, Matilda went to her desk and began to study a text-book on geometry which Miss Honey had given her. The teacher kept half an eye on her all the time and noticed that the child very soon became deeply absorbed in the book. She never glanced up once during the entire lesson.

Miss Honey, meanwhile, was making another decision. She was deciding that she would go herself and have a secret talk with Matilda's mother and father as soon as possible. She simply refused to let the matter rest where it was. The whole thing was ridiculous. She couldn't believe that the parents were totally unaware of their daughter's remarkable talents. After all, Mr Wormwood was a successful motor-car dealer so she presumed that he was a fairly intelligent man himself. In any event, parents never *underestimated* the abilities of their own children. Quite the reverse. Sometimes it was well nigh impossible for a teacher to convince the proud father or mother that their beloved offspring was a complete nitwit. Miss Honey felt confident that she would have no difficulty in convincing Mr and Mrs Wormwood that Matilda was something very special indeed. The trouble was going to be to stop them from getting over-enthusiastic.

And now Miss Honey's hopes began to expand even further. She started wondering whether permission might not be sought from the parents for her to give private tuition to Matilda after school. The prospect of coaching a child as bright as this appealed enormously to her professional instinct as a teacher. And suddenly she decided that she would go and call on Mr and Mrs Wormwood that very evening. She would go fairly late, between nine and ten o'clock, when Matilda was sure to be in bed.

And that is precisely what she did. Having got the address from the school records, Miss Honey set out to walk from her own home to the Wormwood's house shortly after nine. She found the house in a pleasant street where each smallish building was separated from its neighbours by a bit of garden. It was a modern brick house that could not have been cheap to buy and the name on the gate said COSY NOOK. Nosey cook might have been better, Miss Honey thought. She was given to playing with words in that way. She walked up the path and rang the bell, and while she stood waiting she could hear the television blaring inside.

The door was opened by a small ratty-looking man with a thin ratty moustache who was wearing a sports-coat that had an orange and red stripe in the material. "Yes?" he said, peering out at Miss Honey. "If you're selling raffle tickets I don't want any."

"I'm not," Miss Honey said. "And please forgive me for butting in on you like this. I am Matilda's teacher at school and it is important I have a word with you and your wife."

"Got into trouble already, has she?" Mr Wormwood said, blocking the doorway. "Well, she's your
responsibility from now on. You'll have to deal
with her."

"She is in no trouble at all," Miss Honey said. "I have come with good news about her. Quite startling news, Mr Wormwood. Do you think I might come in for a few minutes and talk to you about Matilda?"

"We are right in the middle of watching one of our favourite programmes," Mr Wormwood said. "This is most inconvenient. Why don't you come back some other time."

Miss Honey began to lose patience. "Mr Wormwood," she said, "if you think some rotten TV programme is more important than your daughter's future, then you ought not to be a parent! Why don't you switch the darn thing off and listen to me!"

That shook Mr Wormwood. He was not used to being spoken to in this way. He peered carefully at the slim frail woman who stood so resolutely out on the porch. "Oh very well then," he snapped. "Come on in and let's get it over with." Miss Honey stepped briskly inside.

"Mrs Wormwood isn't going to thank you for this," the man said as he led her into the sitting-room where a large platinum-blonde woman was gazing rapturously at the TV screen.

"Who is it?" the woman said, not looking round.

"Some school teacher," Mr Wormwood said. "She says she's got to talk to us about Matilda." He crossed to the TV set and turned down the sound but left the picture on the screen.

"Don't do that, Harry!" Mrs Wormwood cried out. "Willard is just about to propose to Angelica!"

"You can still watch it while we're talking," Mr Wormwood said. "This is Matilda's teacher. She says she's got some sort of news to give us."

"My name is Jennifer Honey," Miss Honey said. "How do you do, Mrs Wormwood."

Mrs Wormwood glared at her and said, "What's the trouble then?"

Nobody invited Miss Honey to sit down so she chose a chair and sat down anyway. "This", she said, "was your daughter's first day at school."

"We know that," Mrs Wormwood said, ratty about missing her programme. "Is that all you came to tell us?"

Miss Honey stared hard into the other woman's wet grey eyes, and she allowed the silence to hang in the air until Mrs Wormwood became uncomfortable. "Do you wish me to explain why I came?" she said.

"Get on with it then," Mrs Wormwood said.

"I'm sure you know", Miss Honey said, "that children in the bottom class at school are not expected to be able to read or spell or juggle with numbers when they first arrive. Five-year-olds cannot do that. But Matilda can do it all. And if I am to believe her ... "

"I wouldn't," Mrs Wormwood said. She was still ratty at losing the sound on the TV.

"Was she lying, then," Miss Honey said, "when she told me that nobody taught her to multiply or to read? Did either of you teach her?"

"Teach her what?" Mr Wormwood said.

"To read. To read books," Miss Honey said. "Perhaps you *did* teach her. Perhaps she *was* lying. Perhaps you have shelves full of books all over the house. I wouldn't know. Perhaps you are both great readers."

"Of course we read," Mr Wormwood said. "Don't be so daft. I read the *Autocar* and the *Motor* from cover to cover every week."

"This child has already read an astonishing number of books," Miss Honey said. "I was simply trying to find out if she came from a family that loved good literature."

"We don't hold with book-reading," Mr Wormwood said. "You can't make a living from sitting

96

on your fanny and reading story-books. We don't keep them in the house."

"I see," Miss Honey said. "Well, all I came to tell you was that Matilda has a brilliant mind. But I expect you knew that already."

"Of course I knew she could read," the mother said. "She spends her life up in her room buried in some silly book."

"But does it not intrigue you", Miss Honey said, "that a little five-year-old child is reading long adult novels by Dickens and Hemingway? Doesn't that make you jump up and down with excitement?"

"Not particularly," the mother said. "I'm not in favour of blue-stocking girls. A girl should think about making herself look attractive so she can get a good husband later on. Looks is more important than books, Miss Hunky . . . "

"The name is Honey," Miss Honey said.

"Now look at *me*," Mrs Wormwood said. "Then look at *you*. You chose books. I chose looks."

Miss Honey looked at the plain plump person with the smug suet-pudding face who was sitting across the room. "What did you say?" she asked.

"I said you chose books and I chose looks," Mrs Wormwood said. "And who's finished up the better off? Me, of course. I'm sitting pretty in a nice house with a successful businessman and you're left slaving away teaching a lot of nasty little children the ABC."

"Quite right, sugar-plum," Mr Wormwood said, casting a look of such simpering sloppiness at his wife it would have made a cat sick.

Miss Honey decided that if she was going to get anywhere with these people she must not lose her temper. "I haven't told you all of it yet," she said. "Matilda, so far as I can gather at this early stage, is also a kind of mathematical genius. She can multiply complicated figures in her head like lightning."

"What's the point of that when you can buy a calculator?" Mr Wormwood said.

"A girl doesn't get a man by being brainy," Mrs Wormwood said. "Look at that film-star for instance," she added, pointing at the silent TV screen where a bosomy female was being embraced by a craggy actor in the moonlight. "You don't think she got him to do that by multiplying figures at him, do you? Not likely. And now he's going to marry her, you see if he doesn't, and she's going to live in a mansion with a butler and lots of maids."

Miss Honey could hardly believe what she was hearing. She had heard that parents like this existed all over the place and that their children turned out to be delinquents and drop-outs, but it was still a shock to meet a pair of them in the flesh.

"Matilda's trouble", she said, trying once again, "is that she is so far ahead of everyone else around her that it might be worth thinking about some extra kind of private tuition. I seriously believe that she could be brought up to university standard in two or three years with the proper coaching."

"University?" Mr Wormwood shouted, bouncing up in his chair. "Who wants to go to university for heaven's sake! All they learn there is bad habits!"

"That is not true," Miss Honey said. "If you had a heart attack this minute and had to call a doctor, that doctor would be a university graduate. If you got sued for selling someone a rotten second-hand car, you'd have to get a lawyer and he'd be a university graduate, too. Do not despise clever people, Mr Wormwood. But I can see we're not going to agree. I'm sorry I burst in on you like this." Miss Honey rose from her chair and walked out of the room.

Mr Wormwood followed her to the front-door and said, "Good of you to come, Miss Hawkes, or is it Miss Harris?"

"It's neither," Miss Honey said, "but let it go." And away she went.

Throwing the Hammer

The nice thing about Matilda was that if you had met her casually and talked to her you would have thought she was a perfectly normal five-and-a-half-year-old child. She displayed almost no outward signs of her brilliance and she never showed off. "This is a very sensible and quiet little girl," you would have said to yourself. And unless for some reason you had started a discussion with her about literature or mathematics, you would never have known the extent of her brain-power.

It was therefore easy for Matilda to make friends with other children. All those in her class liked her. They knew of course that she was "clever" because they had heard her being questioned by Miss Honey on the first day of term. And they knew also that she was allowed to sit quietly with a book during lessons and not pay attention to the teacher. But children of their age do not search deeply for reasons. They are far too wrapped up in their own small struggles to worry overmuch about what others are doing and why.

Among Matilda's new-found friends was the girl called Lavender. Right from the first day of term the two of them started wandering round together during the morning-break and in the lunch-hour. Lavender was exceptionally small for her age, a skinny little nymph with deep-brown eyes and with dark hair that was cut in a fringe across her forehead. Matilda liked her because she was gutsy and adventurous. She liked Matilda for exactly the same reasons.

Before the first week of term was up, awesome tales about the Headmistress, Miss Trunchbull, began to filter through to the newcomers. Matilda and Lavender, standing in a corner of the playground during morning-break on the third day, were approached by a rugged ten-year-old with a boil on her nose, called Hortensia. "New scum, I suppose," Hortensia said to them, looking down from her great height. She was eating from an extra large bag of potato crisps and digging the stuff out in handfuls. "Welcome to borstal," she added, spraying bits of crisp out of her mouth like snowflakes.

The two tiny ones, confronted by this giant, kept a watchful silence.

"Have you met the Trunchbull yet?" Hortensia asked.

"We've seen her at prayers," Lavender said, "but we haven't met her."

"You've got a treat coming to you," Hortensia said. "She hates very small children. She therefore loathes the bottom class and everyone in it. She thinks five-year-olds are grubs that haven't yet hatched out." In went another fistful of crisps and when she spoke again, out sprayed the crumbs. "If you survive your first year you may just manage to live through the rest of your time here. But many

don't survive. They get carried out on stretchers screaming. I've seen it often." Hortensia paused to observe the effect these remarks were having on the two titchy ones. Not very much. They seemed pretty cool. So the large one decided to regale them with further information.

"I suppose you know the Trunchbull has a lock-up cupboard in her private quarters called The Chokey? Have you heard about The Chokey?"

Matilda and Lavender shook their heads and continued to gaze up at the giant. Being very small, they were inclined to mistrust any creature that was larger than they were, especially senior girls.

"The Chokey", Hortensia went on, "is a very tall but very narrow cupboard. The floor is only ten inches square so you can't sit down or squat in it. You have to stand. And three of the walls are made of cement with bits of broken glass sticking out all over, so you can't lean against them. You have to stand more or less at attention all the time when you get locked up in there. It's terrible."

"Can't you lean against the door?" Matilda asked.

"Don't be daft," Hortensia said. "The door's got thousands of sharp spikey nails sticking out of it. They've been hammered through from the outside, probably by the Trunchbull herself."

"Have you ever been in there?" Lavender asked.

"My first term I was in there six times," Hortensia said. "Twice for a whole day and the other times for two hours each. But two hours is quite bad enough. It's pitch dark and you have to stand up

104

dead straight and if you wobble at all you get spiked
either by the glass on the walls or the nails on the
door.

"Why were you put in?" Matilda asked. "What
had you done?"

"The first time", Hortensia said, "I poured half
a tin of Golden Syrup on to the seat of the chair
the Trunchbull was going to sit on at prayers. It
was wonderful. When she lowered herself into the
chair, there was a loud squelching noise similar to
that made by a hippopotamus when lowering its
foot into the mud on the banks of the Limpopo
River. But you're too small and stupid to have read
the *Just So Stories*, aren't you?"

"I've read them," Matilda said.

"You're a liar," Hortensia said amiably. "You can't even read yet. But no matter. So when the Trunchbull sat down on the Golden Syrup, the squelch was beautiful. And when she jumped up again, the chair sort of stuck to the seat of those awful green breeches she wears and came up with her for a few seconds until the thick syrup slowly came unstuck. Then she clasped her hands to the seat of her breeches and both hands got covered in the muck. You should have heard her bellow."

"But how did she know it was you?" Lavender asked.

"A little squirt called Ollie Bogwhistle sneaked on me," Hortensia said. "I knocked his front teeth out."

"And the Trunchbull put you in The Chokey for a whole day?" Matilda asked, gulping.

"All day long," Hortensia said. "I was off my rocker when she let me out. I was babbling like an idiot."

"What were the other things you did to get put in The Chokey?" Lavender asked.

"Oh I can't remember them all now," Hortensia said. She spoke with the air of an old warrior who has been in so many battles that bravery has become commonplace. "It's all so long ago," she added, stuffing more crisps into her mouth. "Ah yes, I can remember one. Here's what happened. I chose a time when I knew the Trunchbull was out of the way teaching the sixth-formers, and I put up my hand and asked to go to the bogs. But instead of going *there*, I sneaked into the Trunchbull's

room. And after a speedy search I found the drawer where she kept all her gym knickers."

"Go on," Matilda said, spellbound. "What happened next?"

"I had sent away by post, you see, for this very powerful itching-powder," Hortensia said. "It cost 50p a packet and was called The Skin-Scorcher. The label said it was made from the powdered teeth of deadly snakes, and it was guaranteed to raise welts the size of walnuts on your skin. So I sprinkled this stuff inside every pair of knickers in the drawer and then folded them all up again carefully." Hortensia paused to cram more crisps into her mouth.

"Did it work?" Lavender asked.

"Well," Hortensia said, "a few days later, during prayers, the Trunchbull suddenly started scratching herself like mad down below. A-ha, I said to myself. Here we go. She's changed for gym already. It was pretty wonderful to be sitting there watching it all and knowing that I was the only person in the whole school who realised exactly what was going on inside the Trunchbull's pants. And I felt safe, too. I knew I couldn't be caught. Then the scratching got worse. She couldn't stop. She must have thought she had a wasp's nest down there. And then, right in the middle of the Lord's Prayer, she leapt up and grabbed her bottom and rushed out of the room."

Both Matilda and Lavender were enthralled. It was quite clear to them that they were at this moment standing in the presence of a master. Here was somebody who had brought the art of skulduggery to the highest point of perfection, somebody, moreover, who was willing to risk life and limb in pursuit of her calling. They gazed in wonder at this goddess, and suddenly even the boil on her nose was no longer a blemish but a badge of courage.

"But how *did* she catch you that time?" Lavender asked, breathless with wonder.

"She didn't," Hortensia said. "But I got a day in The Chokey just the same."

"Why?" they both asked.

"The Trunchbull", Hortensia said, "has a nasty habit of guessing. When she doesn't know who the culprit is, she makes a guess at it, and the trouble is she's often right. I was the prime suspect this time because of the Golden Syrup job, and although I knew she didn't have any proof, nothing I said made any difference. I kept shouting, 'How could I have done it, Miss Trunchbull? I didn't even know you kept any spare knickers at school! I don't even know what itching-powder is! I've never heard of it!' But the lying didn't help me in spite of the great performance I put on. The Trunchbull simply grabbed me by one ear and rushed me to The Chokey at the double and threw me inside and locked the door. That was my second all-day stretch. It was absolute torture. I was spiked and cut all over when I came out."

"It's like a war," Matilda said, overawed.

"You're darn right it's like a war," Hortensia cried. "And the casualties are terrific. *We* are the crusaders, the gallant army fighting for our lives with hardly any weapons at all and the Trunchbull is the Prince of Darkness, the Foul Serpent, the Fiery Dragon with all the weapons at her command. It's a tough life. We all try to support each other."

"You can rely on us," Lavender said, making her height of three feet two inches stretch as tall as possible.

"No, I can't," Hortensia said. "You're only shrimps. But you never know. We may find a use for you one day in some undercover job."

"Tell us just a little bit more about what she does," Matilda said. "Please do."

"I mustn't frighten you before you've been here a week," Hortensia said.

"You won't," Lavender said. "We may be small but we're quite tough."

"Listen to this then," Hortensia said. "Only yesterday the Trunchbull caught a boy called Julius Rottwinkle eating Liquorice Allsorts during the scripture lesson and she simply picked him up by one arm and flung him clear out of the open classroom window. Our classroom is one floor up and we saw Julius Rottwinkle go sailing out over the garden like a Frisbee and landing with a thump in the middle of the lettuces. Then the Trunchbull turned to us and said, "From now on, anybody caught eating in class goes straight out the window.""

"Did this Julius Rottwinkle break any bones?" Lavender asked.

"Only a few," Hortensia said. "You've got to remember that the Trunchbull once threw the hammer for Britain in the Olympics so she's very proud of her right arm."

"What's throwing the hammer?" Lavender asked.

"The hammer", Hortensia said, "is actually a ruddy great cannon-ball on the end of a long bit of wire, and the thrower whisks it round and round his or her head faster and faster and then lets it go. You have to be terrifically strong. The Trunchbull will throw anything around just to keep her arm in, especially children."

"Good heavens," Lavender said.

"I once heard her say", Hortensia went on, "that a large boy is about the same weight as an Olympic

110

hammer and therefore he's very useful for practising with."

At that point something strange happened. The playground, which up to then had been filled with shrieks and the shouting of children at play, all at once became silent as the grave. "Watch out," Hortensia whispered. Matilda and Lavender glanced round and saw the gigantic figure of Miss Trunchbull advancing through the crowd of boys and girls with menacing strides. The children drew back hastily to let her through and her progress across the asphalt was like that of Moses going through the Red Sea when the waters parted. A formidable figure she was too, in her belted smock and green breeches. Below the knees her calf muscles stood out like grapefruits inside her stockings. "Amanda Thripp!" she was shouting. "You, Amanda Thripp, come here!"

"Hold your hats," Hortensia whispered.

"What's going to happen?" Lavender whispered back.

"That idiot Amanda", Hortensia said, "has let her long hair grow even longer during the hols and her mother has plaited it into pigtails. Silly thing to do."

"Why silly?" Matilda asked.

"If there's one thing the Trunchbull can't stand it's pigtails," Hortensia said.

Matilda and Lavender saw the giant in green breeches advancing upon a girl of about ten who had a pair of plaited golden pigtails hanging over her shoulders. Each pigtail had a blue satin bow at

the end of it and it all looked very pretty. The girl wearing the pigtails, Amanda Thripp, stood quite still, watching the advancing giant, and the expression on her face was one that you might find on the face of a person who is trapped in a small field with an enraged bull which is charging flat-out towards her. The girl was glued to the spot, terror-struck, pop-eyed, quivering, knowing for certain that the Day of Judgment had come for her at last.

Miss Trunchbull had now reached the victim and stood towering over her. "I want those filthy pigtails off before you come back to school tomorrow!" she barked. "Chop 'em off and throw 'em in the dustbin, you understand?"

Amanda, paralysed with fright, managed to stutter, "My m-m-mummy likes them. She p-p-plaits them for me every morning."

"Your mummy's a twit!" the Trunchbull bellowed. She pointed a finger the size of a salami at the child's head and shouted, "You look like a rat with a tail coming out of its head!"

"My m-m-mummy thinks I look lovely, Miss T-T-Trunchbull," Amanda stuttered, shaking like a blancmange.

"I don't give a tinker's toot what your mummy thinks!" the Trunchbull yelled, and with that she lunged forward and grabbed hold of Amanda's pigtails in her right fist and lifted the girl clear off the ground. Then she started swinging her round and round her head, faster and faster and Amanda was screaming blue murder and the Trunchbull was yelling, "I'll give you pigtails, you little rat!"

"Shades of the Olympics," Hortensia murmured. "She's getting up speed now just like she does with the hammer. Ten to one she's going to throw her."

And now the Trunchbull was leaning back against the weight of the whirling girl and

114

pivoting expertly on her toes, spinning round and round, and soon Amanda Thripp was travelling so fast she became a blur, and suddenly, with a mighty grunt, the Trunchbull let go of the pigtails and Amanda went sailing like a rocket right over the wire fence of the playground and high up into the sky.

"Well thrown, sir!" someone shouted from across the playground, and Matilda, who was mesmerised by the whole crazy affair, saw Amanda Thripp descending in a long graceful parabola on to the playing-field beyond. She landed on the grass and bounced three times and finally came to rest. Then, amazingly, she sat up. She looked a trifle dazed and who could blame her, but after a minute or so she was on her feet again and tottering back towards the playground.

The Trunchbull stood in the playground dusting off her hands. "Not bad," she said, "considering I'm not in strict training. Not bad at all." Then she strode away.

"She's mad," Hortensia said.

"But don't the parents complain?" Matilda asked.

"Would yours?" Hortensia asked. "I know mine wouldn't. She treats the mothers and fathers just the same as the children and they're all scared to death of her. I'll be seeing you some time, you two." And with that she sauntered away.

Bruce Bogtrotter
and the Cake

"How can she get *away* with it?" Lavender said to Matilda. "Surely the children go home and tell their mothers and fathers. I know my father would raise a terrific stink if I told him the Headmistress had grabbed me by the hair and slung me over the playground fence."

"No, he wouldn't," Matilda said, "and I'll tell you why. He simply wouldn't believe you."

"Of course he would."

"He wouldn't," Matilda said. "And the reason is obvious. Your story would sound too ridiculous to be believed. And that is the Trunchbull's great secret."

"What is?" Lavender asked.

Matilda said, "Never do anything by halves if you want to get away with it. Be outrageous. Go the whole hog. Make sure everything you do is so completely crazy it's unbelievable. No parent is going to believe this pigtail story, not in a million years. Mine wouldn't. They'd call me a liar."

"In that case", Lavender said, "Amanda's mother isn't going to cut her pigtails off."

"No, she isn't," Matilda said. "Amanda will do it herself. You see if she doesn't."

"Do you think she's mad?" Lavender asked.

"Who?"

"The Trunchbull."

"No, I don't think she's mad," Matilda said. "But she's very dangerous. Being in this school is like being in a cage with a cobra. You have to be very fast on your feet."

They got another example of how dangerous the Headmistress could be on the very next day. During lunch an announcement was made that the whole school should go into the Assembly Hall and be seated as soon as the meal was over.

When all the two hundred and fifty or so boys and girls were settled down in Assembly, the Trunchbull marched on to the platform. None of the other teachers came in with her. She was carrying a riding-crop in her right hand. She stood up there on centre stage in her green breeches with legs apart and riding-crop in hand, glaring at the sea of upturned faces before her.

"What's going to happen?" Lavender whispered.

"I don't know," Matilda whispered back.

The whole school waited for what was coming next.

"Bruce Bogtrotter!" the Trunchbull barked suddenly. "Where is Bruce Bogtrotter?"

A hand shot up among the seated children.

"Come up here!" the Trunchbull shouted. "And look smart about it!"

An eleven-year-old boy who was decidedly large and round stood up and waddled briskly forward. He climbed up on to the platform.

"Stand over there!" the Trunchbull ordered, pointing. The boy stood to one side. He looked

nervous. He knew very well he wasn't up there to be presented with a prize. He was watching the Headmistress with an exceedingly wary eye and he kept edging farther and farther away from her with little shuffles of his feet, rather as a rat might edge away from a terrier that is watching it from across the room. His plump flabby face had turned grey with fearful apprehension. His stockings hung about his ankles.

"This *clot*," boomed the Headmistress, pointing the riding-crop at him like a rapier, "this *blackhead*, this *foul carbuncle*, this *poisonous pustule* that you see before you is none other than a disgusting criminal, a denizen of the underworld, a member of the Mafia!"

"Who, me?" Bruce Bogtrotter said, looking genuinely puzzled.

"A thief!" the Trunchbull screamed. "A crook! A pirate! A brigand! A rustler!"

"Steady on," the boy said. "I mean, dash it all, Headmistress."

"Do you deny it, you miserable little gumboil? Do you plead not guilty?"

"I don't know what you're talking about," the boy said, more puzzled than ever.

"I'll tell you what I'm talking about, you suppurating little blister!" the Trunchbull shouted. "Yesterday morning, during break, you sneaked like a serpent into the kitchen and stole a slice of my private chocolate cake from my tea-tray! That tray had just been prepared for me personally by the cook! It was my morning snack! And as for the cake, it was my own private stock! That was not boy's cake! You don't think for one minute I'm going to eat the filth I give to you? That cake was made from real butter and real cream! And he, that

robber-bandit, that safe-cracker, that highwayman standing over there with his socks around his ankles stole it and ate it!"

"I never did," the boy exclaimed, turning from grey to white.

"Don't lie to me, Bogtrotter!" barked the Trunchbull. "The cook saw you! What's more, she saw you eating it!"

The Trunchbull paused to wipe a fleck of froth from her lips.

When she spoke again her voice was suddenly
softer, quieter, more friendly, and she leaned
towards the boy, smiling. "You like my special
chocolate cake, don't you, Bogtrotter? It's rich and
delicious, isn't it, Bogtrotter?"

"Very good," the boy mumbled. The words were
out before he could stop himself.

"You're right," the Trunchbull said. "It *is* very

good. Therefore I think you should congratulate the cook. When a gentleman has had a particularly good meal, Bogtrotter, he always sends his compliments to the chef. You didn't know that, did you, Bogtrotter? But those who inhabit the criminal underworld are not noted for their good manners."

The boy remained silent.

"Cook!" the Trunchbull shouted, turning her head towards the door. "Come here, cook! Bogtrotter wishes to tell you how good your chocolate cake is!"

The cook, a tall shrivelled female who looked as though all of her body-juices had been dried out of her long ago in a hot oven, walked on to the platform wearing a dirty white apron. Her entrance had clearly been arranged beforehand by the Headmistress.

"Now then, Bogtrotter," the Trunchbull boomed. "Tell cook what you think of her chocolate cake."

"Very good," the boy mumbled. You could see he was now beginning to wonder what all this was leading up to. The only thing he knew for certain was that the law forbade the Trunchbull to hit him with the riding-crop that she kept smacking against her thigh. That was some comfort, but not much because the Trunchbull was totally unpredictable. One never knew what she was going to do next.

"There you are, cook," the Trunchbull cried. "Bogtrotter likes your cake. He adores your cake. Do you have any more of your cake you could give him?"

"I do indeed," the cook said. She seemed to have learnt her lines by heart.

"Then go and get it. And bring a knife to cut it with."

The cook disappeared. Almost at once she was back again staggering under the weight of an enormous round chocolate cake on a china platter. The cake was fully eighteen inches in diameter and it was covered with dark-brown chocolate icing. "Put it on the table," the Trunchbull said.

There was a small table centre stage with a chair behind it. The cook placed the cake carefully on the table. "Sit down, Bogtrotter," the Trunchbull said. "Sit there."

The boy moved cautiously to the table and sat down. He stared at the gigantic cake.

"There you are, Bogtrotter," the Trunchbull said, and once again her voice became soft, persuasive, even gentle. "It's all for you, every bit of it. As you enjoyed that slice you had yesterday so very much, I ordered cook to bake you an extra large one all for yourself."

"Well, thank you," the boy said, totally bemused.

"Thank cook, not me," the Trunchbull said.

"Thank you, cook," the boy said.

The cook stood there like a shrivelled bootlace, tight-lipped, implacable, disapproving. She looked as though her mouth was full of lemon juice.

"Come on then," the Trunchbull said. "Why don't you cut yourself a nice thick slice and try it?"

"What? Now?" the boy said, cautious. He knew

there was a catch in this somewhere, but he wasn't
sure where. "Can't I take it home instead?" he
asked.

"That would be impolite," the Trunchbull said,
with a crafty grin. "You must show cookie here how
grateful you are for all the trouble she's taken."

The boy didn't move.

"Go on, get on with it," the Trunchbull said.
"Cut a slice and taste it. We haven't got all day."

The boy picked up the knife and was about to
cut into the cake when he stopped. He stared at
the cake. Then he looked up at the Trunchbull,
then at the tall stringy cook with her lemon-juice
mouth. All the children in the hall were watching
tensely, waiting for something to happen. They felt
certain it must. The Trunchbull was not a person
who would give someone a whole chocolate cake
to eat just out of kindness. Many were guessing
that it had been filled with pepper or castor-oil or

some other foul-tasting substance that would make the boy violently sick. It might even be arsenic and he would be dead in ten seconds flat. Or perhaps it was a booby-trapped cake and the whole thing would blow up the moment it was cut, taking Bruce Bogtrotter with it. No one in the school put it past the Trunchbull to do any of these things.

"I don't want to eat it," the boy said.

"Taste it, you little brat," the Trunchbull said. "You're insulting the cook."

Very gingerly the boy began to cut a thin slice of the vast cake. Then he levered the slice out. Then he put down the knife and took the sticky thing in his fingers and started very slowly to eat it.

"It's good, isn't it?" the Trunchbull asked.

"Very good," the boy said, chewing and swallowing. He finished the slice.

"Have another," the Trunchbull said.

"That's enough, thank you," the boy murmured.

"I said have another," the Trunchbull said, and now there was an altogether sharper edge to her voice. "Eat another slice! Do as you are told!"

"I don't want another slice," the boy said.

Suddenly the Trunchbull exploded. "Eat!" she shouted, banging her thigh with the riding-crop. "If I tell you to eat, you will eat! You wanted cake! You stole cake! And now you've got cake! What's more, you're going to eat it! You do not leave this platform and nobody leaves this hall until you have eaten the entire cake that is sitting there in front of you! Do I make myself clear, Bogtrotter? Do you get my meaning?"

127

The boy looked at the Trunchbull. Then he looked down at the enormous cake.

"Eat! Eat! Eat!" the Trunchbull was yelling.

Very slowly the boy cut himself another slice and began to eat it.

Matilda was fascinated. "Do you think he can do it?" she whispered to Lavender.

"No," Lavender whispered back. "It's impossible. He'd be sick before he was halfway through."

The boy kept going. When he had finished the second slice, he looked at the Trunchbull, hesitating.

"Eat!" she shouted. "Greedy little thieves who like to eat cake must have cake! Eat faster boy! Eat faster! We don't want to be here all day! And don't stop like you're doing now! Next time you stop before it's all finished you'll go straight into The Chokey and I shall lock the door and throw the key down the well!"

The boy cut a third slice and started to eat it. He finished this one quicker than the other two and when that was done he immediately picked up the knife and cut the next slice. In some peculiar way he seemed to be getting into his stride.

Matilda, watching closely, saw no signs of distress in the boy yet. If anything, he seemed to be gathering confidence as he went along. "He's doing well," she whispered to Lavender.

"He'll be sick soon," Lavender whispered back. "It's going to be horrid."

When Bruce Bogtrotter had eaten his way through half of the entire enormous cake, he

128

paused for just a couple of seconds and took several deep breaths.

The Trunchbull stood with hands on hips, glaring at him. "Get on with it!" she shouted. "Eat it up!"

Suddenly the boy let out a gigantic belch which rolled around the Assembly Hall like thunder. Many of the audience began to giggle.

"Silence!" shouted the Trunchbull.

The boy cut himself another thick slice and started eating it fast. There were still no signs of flagging or giving up. He certainly did not look as though he was about to stop and cry out, "I can't, I can't eat any more! I'm going to be sick!" He was still in there running.

And now a subtle change was coming over the two hundred and fifty watching children in the audience. Earlier on, they had sensed impending disaster. They had prepared themselves for an unpleasant scene in which the wretched boy, stuffed to the gills with chocolate cake, would have to surrender and beg for mercy and then they would have watched the triumphant Trunchbull forcing more and still more cake into the mouth of the gasping boy.

Not a bit of it. Bruce Bogtrotter was three-quarters of the way through and still going strong. One sensed that he was almost beginning to enjoy himself. He had a mountain to climb and he was jolly well going to reach the top or die in the attempt. What is more, he had now become very conscious of his audience and of how they were all silently rooting for him. This was nothing less than a battle between him and the mighty Trunchbull.

Suddenly someone shouted, "Come on Brucie! You can make it!"

The Trunchbull wheeled round and yelled, "Silence!" The audience watched intently. They were thoroughly caught up in the contest. They were longing to start cheering but they didn't dare.

"I think he's going to make it," Matilda whispered.

"I think so too," Lavender whispered back. "I wouldn't have believed anyone in the world could eat the whole of a cake that size."

"The Trunchbull doesn't believe it either," Matilda whispered. "Look at her. She's turning redder and redder. She's going to kill him if he wins."

The boy was slowing down now. There was no

doubt about that. But he kept pushing the stuff
into his mouth with the dogged perseverance of a
long-distance runner who has sighted the
finishing-line and knows he must keep going. As
the very last mouthful disappeared, a tremendous
cheer rose up from the audience and children were
leaping on to their chairs and yelling and clapping
and shouting, "Well done, Brucie! Good for you,
Brucie! You've won a gold medal, Brucie!"

The Trunchbull stood motionless on the platform. Her great horsy face had turned the colour of molten lava and her eyes were glittering with fury. She glared at Bruce Bogtrotter who was sitting on his chair like some huge overstuffed grub, replete, comatose, unable to move or to speak. A fine sweat was beading his forehead but there was a grin of triumph on his face.

Suddenly the Trunchbull lunged forward and grabbed the large empty china platter on which the cake had rested. She raised it high in the air and brought it down with a crash right on the top of the wretched Bruce Bogtrotter's head and pieces flew all over the platform.

The boy was by now so full of cake he was like a sackful of wet cement and you couldn't have hurt him with a sledge-hammer. He simply shook his head a few times and went on grinning.

"Go to blazes!" screamed the Trunchbull and she marched off the platform followed closely by the cook.

Lavender

In the middle of the first week of Matilda's first term, Miss Honey said to the class, "I have some important news for you, so listen carefully. You too, Matilda. Put that book down for a moment and pay attention."

Small eager faces looked up and listened.

"It is the Headmistress's custom", Miss Honey went on, "to take over the class for one period each week. She does this with every class in the school and each class has a fixed day and a fixed time. Ours is always two o'clock on Thursday afternoons, immediately after lunch. So tomorrow at two o'clock Miss Trunchbull will be taking over from me for one lesson. I shall be here as well, of course, but only as a silent witness. Is that understood?"

"Yes, Miss Honey," they chirruped.

"A word of warning to you all," Miss Honey said. "The Headmistress is very strict about everything. Make sure your clothes are clean, your faces are clean and your hands are clean. Speak only when spoken to. When she asks you a question, stand up at once before you answer it. Never argue with her. Never answer back. Never try to be funny. If you do, you will make her angry, and when the Headmistress gets angry you had better watch out."

"You can say that again," Lavender murmured.

"I am quite sure", Miss Honey said, "that she will be testing you on what you are meant to have learnt this week, which is your two-times table. So I strongly advise you to swot it up when you get home tonight. Get your mother or father to hear you on it."

"What else will she test us on?" someone asked.

"Spelling," Miss Honey said. "Try to remember everything you have learned these last few days. And one more thing. A jug of water and a glass must always be on the table here when the Headmistress comes in. She never takes a lesson without that. Now who will be responsible for seeing that it's there?"

"I will," Lavender said at once.

"Very well, Lavender," Miss Honey said. "It will be your job to go to the kitchen and get the jug and fill it with water and put it on the table here with a clean empty glass just before the lesson starts."

"What if the jug's not in the kitchen?" Lavender asked.

"There are a dozen Headmistress's jugs and glasses in the kitchen," Miss Honey said. "They are used all over the school."

"I won't forget," Lavender said. "I promise I won't."

Already Lavender's scheming mind was going over the possibilities that this water-jug job had opened up for her. She longed to do something truly heroic. She admired the older girl Hortensia to distraction for the daring deeds she had performed in the school. She also admired Matilda who had sworn her to secrecy about the parrot job she had brought off at home, and also the great hair-oil switch which had bleached her father's hair. It was *her* turn now to become a heroine if only she could come up with a brilliant plot.

On the way home from school that afternoon

136

she began to mull over the various possibilities, and when at last the germ of a brilliant idea hit her, she began to expand on it and lay her plans with the same kind of care the Duke of Wellington had done before the Battle of Waterloo. Admittedly the enemy on this occasion was not Napoleon. But you would never have got anyone at Crunchem Hall to admit that the Headmistress was a less formidable foe than the famous Frenchman. Great skill would have to be exercised, Lavender told herself, and great secrecy observed if she was to come out of this exploit alive.

There was a muddy pond at the bottom of Lavender's garden and this was the home of a colony of newts. The newt, although fairly common in English ponds, is not often seen by ordinary people because it is a shy and murky creature. It is an incredibly ugly gruesome-looking animal, rather like a baby crocodile but with a shorter head. It is quite harmless but doesn't look it. It is about six inches long and very slimy, with a greenish-grey skin on top and an orange-coloured belly underneath. It is, in fact, an amphibian, which can live in or out of water.

That evening Lavender went to the bottom of the garden determined to catch a newt. They are swiftly-moving animals and not easy to get hold of. She lay on the bank for a long time waiting patiently until she spotted a whopper. Then, using her school hat as a net, she swooped and caught it. She had lined her pencil-box with pond-weed ready to receive the creature, but she discovered that it

was not easy to get the newt out of the hat and into the pencil-box. It wriggled and squirmed like quicksilver and, apart from that, the box was only just long enough to take it. When she did get it in at last, she had to be careful not to trap its tail in the lid when she slid it closed. A boy next door called Rupert Entwistle had told her that if you chopped off a newt's tail, the tail stayed alive and grew into another newt ten times bigger than the first one. It could be the size of an alligator. Lavender didn't quite believe that, but she was not prepared to risk it happening.

Eventually she managed to slide the lid of the pencil-box right home and the newt was hers. Then, on second thoughts, she opened the lid just the tiniest fraction so that the creature could breathe.

The next day she carried her secret weapon to school in her satchel. She was tingling with excitement. She was longing to tell Matilda about her plan of battle. In fact, she wanted to tell the whole class. But she finally decided to tell nobody. It was better that way because then no one, even when put under the most severe torture, would be able to name her as the culprit.

Lunchtime came. Today it was sausages and baked beans, Lavender's favourite, but she couldn't eat it.

"Are you feeling all right, Lavender?" Miss Honey asked from the head of the table.

"I had such a huge breakfast", Lavender said, "I really couldn't eat a thing."

139

Immediately after lunch, she dashed off to the kitchen and found one of the Trunchbull's famous jugs. It was a large bulging thing made of blue-glazed pottery. Lavender filled it half-full of water and carried it, together with a glass, into the class-room and set it on the teacher's table. The class-room was still empty. Quick as a flash, Lavender got her pencil-box from her satchel and slid open the lid just a tiny bit. The newt was lying quite still. With great care, she held the box over the neck of the jug and pulled the lid fully open and tipped the newt in. There was a plop as it landed in the water, then it thrashed around wildly for a few seconds before settling down. And now, to make the newt feel more at home, Lavender decided to give it all the pond-weed from the pencil-box as well.

The deed was done. All was ready. Lavender put her pencils back into the rather damp pencil-box and returned it to its correct place on her own desk. Then she went out and joined the others in the playground until it was time for the lesson to begin.

140

The Weekly Test

At two o'clock sharp the class assembled, including Miss Honey who noted that the jug of water and the glass were in the proper place. Then she took up a position standing right at the back. Everyone waited. Suddenly in marched the gigantic figure of the Headmistress in her belted smock and green breeches.

"Good afternoon, children," she barked.

"Good afternoon, Miss Trunchbull," they chirruped.

The Headmistress stood before the class, legs apart, hands on hips, glaring at the small boys and girls who sat nervously at their desks in front of her.

"*Not* a very pretty sight," she said. Her expression was one of utter distaste, as though she were looking at something a dog had done in the middle of the floor. "What a bunch of nauseating little warts you are."

Everyone had the sense to stay silent.

"It makes me vomit", she went on, "to think that I am going to have to put up with a load of garbage like you in my school for the next six years. I can see that I'm going to have to expel as many of you as possible as soon as possible to save myself from going round the bend." She paused and snorted several times. It was a curious noise. You can hear the same sort of thing if you walk through a riding-stable when the horses are being fed. "I suppose", she went on, "your mothers and fathers tell you you're wonderful. Well, I am here to tell you the opposite, and you'd better believe me. Stand up everybody!"

They all got quickly to their feet.

"Now put your hands out in front of you. And as I walk past I want you to turn them over so I can see if they are clean on both sides."

The Trunchbull began a slow march along the rows of desks inspecting the hands. All went well until she came to a small boy in the second row. "What's your name?" she barked.

"Nigel," the boy said.

"Nigel what?"

"Nigel Hicks," the boy said.

"Nigel Hicks what?" the Trunchbull bellowed. She bellowed so loud she nearly blew the little chap out of the window.

"That's it," Nigel said. "Unless you want my middle names as well." He was a brave little fellow and one could see that he was trying not to be scared by the Gorgon who towered above him.

"I do *not* want your middle names, you blister!" the Gorgon bellowed. "What is *my* name?"

"Miss Trunchbull," Nigel said.

"Then use it when you address me! Now then, let's try again. What is your name?"

"Nigel Hicks, Miss Trunchbull," Nigel said.

"That's better," the Trunchbull said. "Your

142

hands are filthy, Nigel! When did you last wash them?''

"Well, let me think," Nigel said. "That's rather difficult to remember exactly. It could have been yesterday or it could have been the day before."

The Trunchbull's whole body and face seemed to swell up as though she were being inflated by a bicycle-pump.

"I knew it!" she bellowed. "I knew as soon as I saw you that you were nothing but a piece of filth! What is your father's job, a sewage-worker?"

"He's a doctor," Nigel said. "And a jolly good one. He says we're all so covered with bugs anyway that a bit of extra dirt never hurts anyone."

"I'm glad he's not *my* doctor," the Trunchbull said. "And why, might I ask, is there a baked bean on the front of your shirt?"

"We had them for lunch, Miss Trunchbull."

"And do you usually put your lunch on the front of your shirt, Nigel? Is that what this famous doctor father of yours has taught you to do?"

"Baked beans are hard to eat, Miss Trunchbull. They keep falling off my fork."

"You are disgusting!" the Trunchbull bellowed. "You are a walking germ-factory! I don't wish to see any more of you today! Go and stand in the corner on one leg with your face to the wall!"

"But Miss Trunchbull . . . "

"Don't argue with me, boy, or I'll make you stand on your head! Now do as you're told!"

Nigel went.

"Now stay where you are, boy, while I test you on your spelling to see if you've learnt anything at all this past week. And don't turn round when you talk to me. Keep your nasty little face to the wall. Now then, spell 'write'."

"Which one?" Nigel asked. "The thing you do

with a pen or the one that means the opposite of wrong?" He happened to be an unusually bright child and his mother had worked hard with him at home on spelling and reading.

"The one with the pen, you little fool."

Nigel spelled it correctly which surprised the Trunchbull. She thought she had given him a very tricky word, one that he wouldn't yet have learned, and she was peeved that he had succeeded.

Then Nigel said, still balancing on one leg and facing the wall, "Miss Honey taught us how to spell a new very long word yesterday."

"And what word was that?" the Trunchbull asked softly. The softer her voice became, the greater the danger, but Nigel wasn't to know this.

"'Difficulty'," Nigel said. "Everyone in the class can spell 'difficulty' now."

"What nonsense," the Trunchbull said. "You are not supposed to learn long words like that until you are at least eight or nine. And don't try to tell me *everybody* in the class can spell that word. You are lying to me, Nigel."

"Test someone," Nigel said, taking an awful chance. "Test anyone you like."

The Trunchbull's dangerous glittering eyes roved around the class-room. "You," she said, pointing at a tiny and rather daft little girl called Prudence, "Spell 'difficulty'."

Amazingly, Prudence spelled it correctly and without a moment's hesitation.

The Trunchbull was properly taken aback. "Humph!" she snorted. "And I suppose Miss Honey wasted the whole of one lesson teaching you to spell that one single word?"

"Oh no, she didn't," piped Nigel. "Miss Honey taught it to us in three minutes so we'll never

146

forget it. She teaches us lots of words in three minutes."

"And what exactly is this magic method, Miss Honey?" asked the Headmistress.

"I'll show you," piped up the brave Nigel again, coming to Miss Honey's rescue. "Can I put my other foot down and turn round, please, while I show you?"

"You may do neither!" snapped the Trunchbull. "Stay as you are and show me just the same!"

"All right," said Nigel, wobbling crazily on his one leg. "Miss Honey gives us a little song about each word and we all sing it together and we learn to spell it in no time. Would you like to hear the song about 'difficulty'?"

"I should be fascinated," the Trunchbull said in a voice dripping with sarcasm.

"Here it is," Nigel said.

"Mrs D, Mrs I, Mrs FFI
Mrs C, Mrs U, Mrs LTY.

That spells difficulty."

"How perfectly ridiculous!" snorted the Trunchbull. "Why are all these women married? And anyway you're not meant to teach poetry when you're teaching spelling. Cut it out in future, Miss Honey."

"But it does teach them some of the harder words wonderfully well," Miss Honey murmured.

"Don't argue with me, Miss Honey!" the Headmistress thundered. "Just do as you're told! I shall now test the class on the multiplication tables to see if Miss Honey has taught you anything at all in that direction." The Trunchbull had returned to her place in front of the class, and her diabolical gaze was moving slowly along the rows of tiny pupils. "You!" she barked, pointing at a small boy called Rupert in the front row. "What is two sevens?"

"Sixteen," Rupert answered with foolish abandon.

The Trunchbull started advancing slow and soft-footed upon Rupert in the manner of a tigress stalking a small deer. Rupert suddenly became aware of the danger signals and quickly tried again. "It's eighteen!" he cried. "Two sevens are eighteen, not sixteen!"

"You ignorant little slug!" the Trunchbull bellowed. "You witless weed! You empty-headed hamster! You stupid glob of glue!" She had now stationed herself directly behind Rupert, and suddenly she extended a hand the size of a tennis racquet and grabbed all the hair on Rupert's head in her fist. Rupert had a lot of golden-coloured hair. His mother thought it was beautiful to behold and took a delight in allowing it to grow extra long. The Trunchbull had as great a dislike for long hair on boys as she had for plaits and pigtails on girls and she was about to show it. She took a firm grip on Rupert's long golden tresses with her giant hand and then, by raising her muscular right arm, she lifted the helpless boy clean out of his chair and held him aloft.

148

Rupert yelled. He twisted and squirmed and kicked the air and went on yelling like a stuck pig, and Miss Trunchbull bellowed, "Two sevens are fourteen! Two sevens are fourteen! I am not letting you go till you say it!"

From the back of the class, Miss Honey cried out, "Miss Trunchbull! Please let him down! You're hurting him! All his hair might come out!"

"And well it might if he doesn't stop wriggling!" snorted the Trunchbull. "Keep still, you squirming worm!"

It really was a quite extraordinary sight to see this giant Headmistress dangling the small boy high in the air and the boy spinning and twisting like something on the end of a string and shrieking his head off.

"Say it!" bellowed the Trunchbull. "Say two sevens are fourteen! Hurry up or I'll start jerking you up and down and then your hair really will come out and we'll have enough of it to stuff a sofa! Get on with it boy! Say two sevens are fourteen and I'll let you go!"

"T-t-two s-sevens are f-f-fourteen," gasped Rupert, whereupon the Trunchbull, true to her word, opened her hand and quite literally let him go. He was a long way off the ground when she released him and he plummeted to earth and hit the floor and bounced like a football.

"Get up and stop whimpering," the Trunchbull barked.

Rupert got up and went back to his desk massaging his scalp with both hands. The Trunchbull returned to the front of the class. The children sat there hypnotised. None of them had seen anything quite like this before. It was splendid entertain-

150

ment. It was better than a pantomime, but with one big difference. In this room there was an enormous human bomb in front of them which was liable to explode and blow someone to bits any moment. The children's eyes were riveted on the Headmistress. "I don't like small people," she was saying. "Small people should never be seen by anybody. They should be kept out of sight in boxes like hairpins and buttons. I cannot for the life of me see why children have to take so long to grow up. I think they do it on purpose."

Another extremely brave little boy in the front row spoke up and said, "But surely *you* were a small person once, Miss Trunchbull, weren't you?"

"I was *never* a small person," she snapped. "I have been large all my life and I don't see why others can't be the same way."

"But you must have started out as a baby," the boy said.

"*Me!* A baby!" shouted the Trunchbull. "How dare you suggest such a thing! What cheek! What infernal insolence! What's your name, boy? And stand up when you speak to me!"

The boy stood up. "My name is Eric Ink, Miss Trunchbull," he said.

"Eric *what*?" the Trunchbull shouted.

"Ink," the boy said.

"Don't be an ass, boy! There's no such name!"

"Look in the phone book," Eric said. "You'll see my father there under Ink."

"Very well, then," the Trunchbull said, "You may be Ink, young man, but let me tell you something. You're not indelible. I'll very soon rub you out if you try getting clever with me. Spell what."

"I don't understand," Eric said. "What do you want me to spell?"

"Spell what, you idiot! Spell the word 'what'!"

"W . . . O . . . T," Eric said, answering too quickly.

There was a nasty silence.

"I'll give you one more chance," the Trunchbull said, not moving.

"Ah yes, I know," Eric said. "It's got an H in it. W . . . H . . . O . . . T. It's easy."

In two large strides the Trunchbull was behind Eric's desk, and there she stood, a pillar of doom towering over the helpless boy. Eric glanced fearfully back over his shoulder at the monster. "I *was* right, wasn't I?" he murmured nervously.

"You were *wrong*!" the Trunchbull barked. "In fact you strike me as the sort of poisonous little pockmark that will *always* be wrong! You sit wrong! You look wrong! You speak wrong! You are wrong all round! I will give you one more chance to be right! Spell 'what'!"

Eric hesitated. Then he said very slowly, "It's not W . . . O . . . T, and it's not W . . . H . . . O . . . T. Ah, I know. It must be W . . . H . . . O . . . T . . . T."

Standing behind Eric, the Trunchbull reached out and took hold of the boy's two ears, one with each hand, pinching them between forefinger and thumb.

"Ow!" Eric cried. "Ow! You're hurting me!"

"I haven't started yet," the Trunchbull said briskly. And now, taking a firm grip on his two ears, she lifted him bodily out of his seat and held him aloft.

Like Rupert before him, Eric squealed the house down.

From the back of the class-room Miss Honey cried out, "Miss Trunchbull! Don't! Please let him go! His ears might come off!"

"They'll never come off," the Trunchbull

shouted back. "I have discovered through long experience, Miss Honey, that the ears of small boys are stuck very firmly to their heads."

"Let him go, Miss Trunchbull, please," begged Miss Honey. "You could damage him, you really could! You could wrench them right off!"

"Ears never come off!" the Trunchbull shouted. "They stretch most marvellously, like these are doing now, but I can assure you they never come off!"

Eric was squealing louder than ever and pedalling the air with his legs.

Matilda had never before seen a boy, or anyone else for that matter, held aloft by his ears alone. Like Miss Honey, she felt sure both ears were going to come off at any moment with all the weight that was on them.

The Trunchbull was shouting, "The word 'what' is spelled W . . . H . . . A . . . T. Now spell it, you little wart!"

Eric didn't hesitate. He had learned from watching Rupert a few minutes before that the quicker you answered the quicker you were released. "W . . . H . . . A . . . T", he squealed, "spells what!"

Still holding him by the ears, the Trunchbull lowered him back into his chair behind his desk. Then she marched back to the front of the class, dusting off her hands one against the other like someone who has been handling something rather grimy.

"That's the way to make them learn, Miss Honey," she said. "You take it from me, it's no good just *telling* them. You've got to *hammer* it into them. There's nothing like a little twisting and twiddling to encourage them to remember things. It concentrates their minds wonderfully."

"You could do them permanent damage, Miss Trunchbull," Miss Honey cried out.

"Oh, I have, I'm quite sure I have," the Trunchbull answered, grinning. "Eric's ears will have stretched quite considerably in the last couple of minutes! They'll be much longer now than they were before. There's nothing wrong with that, Miss Honey. It'll give him an interesting pixie look for the rest of his life."

"But Miss Trunchbull . . . "

"Oh, do shut up, Miss Honey! You're as wet as any of them. If you can't cope in here then you can go and find a job in some cotton-wool private school

155

for rich brats. When you have been teaching for as long as I have you'll realise that it's no good at all being kind to children. Read *Nicholas Nickleby*, Miss Honey, by Mr Dickens. Read about Mr Wackford Squeers, the admirable headmaster of Dotheboys Hall. *He* knew how to handle the little brutes, didn't he! He knew how to use the birch, didn't he! He kept their backsides so warm you could have fried eggs and bacon on them! A fine book, that. But I don't suppose this bunch of morons we've got here will ever read it because by the look of them they are never going to learn to read any thing!"

"I've read it," Matilda said quietly.

The Trunchbull flicked her head round and looked carefully at the small girl with dark hair and deep brown eyes sitting in the second row. "What did you say?" she asked sharply.

"I said I've read it, Miss Trunchbull."

"Read what?"

"*Nicholas Nickleby*, Miss Trunchbull."

"You are lying to me, madam!" the Trunchbull shouted, glaring at Matilda. "I doubt there is a single child in the entire school who has read that book, and here you are, an unhatched shrimp sitting in the lowest form there is, trying to tell me a whopping great lie like that! Why do you do it? You must take me for a fool! Do you take me for a fool, child?"

"Well . . . " Matilda said, then she hesitated. She would like to have said, "Yes, I jolly well do," but that would have been suicide. "Well . . . " she said

again, still hesitating, still refusing to say "No".

The Trunchbull sensed what the child was thinking and she didn't like it. "Stand up when you speak to me!" she snapped. "What is your name?"

Matilda stood up and said, "My name is Matilda Wormwood, Miss Trunchbull."

"Wormwood, is it?" the Trunchbull said. "In

that case you must be the daughter of that man who owns Wormwood Motors?"

"Yes, Miss Trunchbull."

"He's a crook!" the Trunchbull shouted. "A week ago he sold me a second-hand car that he said was almost new. I thought he was a splendid fellow then. But this morning, while I was driving that car through the village, the entire engine fell out on to the road! The whole thing was filled with sawdust! The man's a thief and a robber! I'll have his skin for sausages, you see if I don't!"

"He's clever at his business," Matilda said.

"Clever my foot!" the Trunchbull shouted. "Miss Honey tells me that *you* are meant to be clever, too! Well madam, I don't like clever people! They are all crooked! *You* are most certainly crooked! Before I fell out with your father, he told me some very nasty stories about the way you behaved at home! But you'd better not try anything in this school, young lady. I shall be keeping a very careful eye on you from now on. Sit down and keep quiet."

The First Miracle

Matilda sat down again at her desk. The Trunchbull seated herself behind the teacher's table. It
was the first time she had sat down during the
lesson. Then she reached out a hand and took hold
of her water-jug. Still holding the jug by the handle
but not lifting it yet, she said, "I have never been
able to understand why small children are so disgusting. They are the bane of my life. They are
like insects. They should be got rid of as early as
possible. We get rid of flies with fly-spray and
by hanging up fly-paper. I have often thought of
inventing a spray for getting rid of small children.
How splendid it would be to walk into this class-
room with a gigantic spray-gun in my hands and
start pumping it. Or better still, some huge strips
of sticky paper. I would hang them all round the
school and you'd all get stuck to them and that
would be the end of it. Wouldn't that be a good
idea, Miss Honey?"

"If it's meant to be a joke, Headmistress, I don't
think it's a very funny one," Miss Honey said from
the back of the class.

"You wouldn't, would you, Miss Honey," the
Trunchbull said. "And it's *not* meant to be a joke.
My idea of a perfect school, Miss Honey, is one
that has no children in it at all. One of these days

I shall start up a school like that. I think it will be very successful."

The woman's mad, Miss Honey was telling herself. She's round the twist. She's the one who ought to be got rid of.

The Trunchbull now lifted the large blue porcelain water-jug and poured some water into her glass. And suddenly, with the water, out came the long slimy newt straight into the glass, *plop*!

The Trunchbull let out a yell and leapt off her chair as though a firecracker had gone off underneath her. And now the children also saw the long thin slimy yellow-bellied lizard-like creature twisting and turning in the glass, and they squirmed and jumped about as well, shouting, "What is it? Oh, it's disgusting! It's a snake! It's a baby crocodile! It's an alligator!"

"Look out, Miss Trunchbull!" cried Lavender. "I'll bet it bites!"

The Trunchbull, this mighty female giant, stood there in her green breeches, quivering like a blancmange. She was especially furious that someone had succeeded in making her jump and yell like that because she prided herself on her toughness. She stared at the creature twisting and wriggling in the glass. Curiously enough, she had never seen a newt before. Natural history was not her strong point. She hadn't the faintest idea what this thing was. It certainly looked extremely unpleasant. Slowly she sat down again in her chair. She looked at this moment more terrifying than ever before. The fires of fury and hatred were smouldering in her small black eyes.

"Matilda!" she barked. "Stand up!"

"Who, me?" Matilda said. "What have I done?"

"Stand up, you disgusting little cockroach!"

"I haven't done anything, Miss Trunchbull, honestly I haven't. I've never seen that slimy thing before!"

"Stand up at once, you filthy little maggot!"

Reluctantly, Matilda got to her feet. She was in

the second row. Lavender was in the row behind her, feeling a bit guilty. She hadn't intended to get her friend into trouble. On the other hand, she was certainly not about to own up.

"You are a vile, repulsive, repellent, malicious little brute!" the Trunchbull was shouting. "You are not fit to be in this school! You ought to be behind bars, that's where you ought to be! I shall have you drummed out of this establishment in utter disgrace! I shall have the prefects chase you down the corridor and out of the front-door with hockey-sticks! I shall have the staff escort you home under armed guard! And then I shall make absolutely sure you are sent to a reformatory for delinquent girls for the minimum of forty years!"

The Trunchbull was in such a rage that her face had taken on a boiled colour and little flecks of froth were gathering at the corners of her mouth. But she was not the only one who was losing her cool. Matilda was also beginning to see red. She didn't in the least mind being accused of having done something she had actually done. She could see the justice of that. It was, however, a totally new experience for her to be accused of a crime that she definitely had not committed. She had had absolutely nothing to do with that beastly creature in the glass. By golly, she thought, that rotten Trunchbull isn't going to pin this one on me!

"I did not do it!" she screamed.

162

"Oh yes, you did!" the Trunchbull roared back.
"Nobody else could have thought up a trick like
that! Your father was right to warn me about you!"
The woman seemed to have lost control of herself
completely. She was ranting like a maniac. "You
are finished in this school, young lady!" she
shouted. "You are finished everywhere. I shall personally see to it that you are put away in a place
where not even the crows can land their droppings
on you! You will probably never see the light of
day again!"

"*I'm telling you I did not do it!*" Matilda
screamed. "I've never even seen a creature like that
in my life!"

"You have put a . . . a . . . a crocodile in my drinking water!" the Trunchbull yelled back. "There is no worse crime in the world against a Headmistress! Now sit down and don't say a word! Go on, sit down at once!"

"*But I'm telling you* . . . " Matilda shouted, refusing to sit down.

"I am telling you to shut up!" the Trunchbull roared. "If you don't shut up at once and sit down I shall remove my belt and let you have it with the end that has the buckle!"

Slowly Matilda sat down. Oh, the rottenness of it all! The unfairness! How dare they expel her for something she hadn't done!

Matilda felt herself getting angrier . . . and angrier . . . and angrier . . . so unbearably angry that something was bound to explode inside her very soon.

The newt was still squirming in the tall glass of water. It looked horribly uncomfortable. The glass was not big enough for it. Matilda glared at the Trunchbull. How she hated her. She glared at the glass with the newt in it. She longed to march up and grab the glass and tip the contents, newt and all, over the Trunchbull's head. She trembled to think what the Trunchbull would do to her if she did that.

The Trunchbull was sitting behind the teacher's table staring with a mixture of horror and fascination at the newt wriggling in the glass. Matilda's eyes were also riveted on the glass. And now, quite slowly, there began to creep over Matilda a most

164

extraordinary and peculiar feeling. The feeling was mostly in the eyes. A kind of electricity seemed to be gathering inside them. A sense of power was brewing in those eyes of hers, a feeling of great strength was settling itself deep inside her eyes. But there was also another feeling which was something else altogether, and which she could not understand. It was like flashes of lightning. Little waves of lightning seemed to be flashing out of her eyes. Her eyeballs were beginning to get hot, as though vast energy was building up somewhere inside them. It was an amazing sensation. She kept her eyes steadily on the glass, and now the power was concentrating itself in one small part of each eye and growing stronger and stronger and it felt as though millions of tiny little invisible arms with hands on them were shooting out of her eyes towards the glass she was staring at.

"Tip it!" Matilda whispered. *"Tip it over!"*

She saw the glass wobble. It actually tilted backwards a fraction of an inch, then righted itself again. She kept pushing at it with all those millions of invisible little arms and hands that were reaching out from her eyes, feeling the power that was flashing straight from the two little black dots in the very centres of her eyeballs.

"Tip it!" she whispered again. *"Tip it over!"*

Once more the glass wobbled. She pushed harder still, willing her eyes to shoot out more power. And then, very very slowly, so slowly she could hardly see it happening, the glass began to lean backwards, farther and farther and farther backwards until it was balancing on just one edge of its base. And there it teetered for a few seconds before finally toppling over and falling with a sharp tinkle on to the desk-top. The water in it and the squirming newt splashed out all over Miss Trunchbull's enormous bosom. The headmistress let out a yell that must have rattled every window-pane in the building and for the second time in the last five minutes she shot out of her chair like a rocket. The newt clutched desperately at the cotton smock where it covered the great chest and there it clung with its little claw-like feet. The Trunchbull looked down and saw it and she bellowed even louder and with a swipe of her hand she sent the creature flying across the class-room. It landed on the floor beside Lavender's desk and very quickly she ducked down and picked it up and put it into her pencil-box for another time. A newt, she decided, was a useful thing to have around.

The Trunchbull, her face more like a boiled ham than ever, was standing before the class quivering with fury. Her massive bosom was heaving in and out and the splash of water down the front of it

made a dark wet patch that had probably soaked right through to her skin.

"*Who did it?*" she roared. "*Come on! Own up! Step forward! You won't escape this time! Who is responsible for this dirty job? Who pushed over this glass?*"

Nobody answered. The whole room remained silent as a tomb.

"Matilda!" she roared. "It was you! I know it was you!"

Matilda, in the second row, sat very still and said nothing. A strange feeling of serenity and confidence was sweeping over her and all of a sudden she found that she was frightened by nobody in the world. With the power of her eyes alone she had compelled a glass of water to tip and spill its contents over the horrible Headmistress, and anybody who could do that could do anything.

"Speak up, you clotted carbuncle!" roared the Trunchbull. "Admit that you did it!"

Matilda looked right back into the flashing eyes of this infuriated female giant and said with total calmness, "I have not moved away from my desk, Miss Trunchbull, since the lesson began. I can say no more."

Suddenly the entire class seemed to rise up against the Headmistress. "She didn't move!" they cried out. "Matilda didn't move! Nobody moved! You must have knocked it over yourself!"

"I most certainly did not knock it over myself!" roared the Trunchbull. "How dare you suggest a thing like that! Speak up, Miss Honey! You must have seen everything! Who knocked over my glass?"

"None of the children did, Miss Trunchbull," Miss Honey answered. "I can vouch for it that nobody has moved from his or her desk all the time you've been here, except for Nigel and he has not moved from his corner."

Miss Trunchbull glared at Miss Honey. Miss Honey met her gaze without flinching. "I am telling you the truth, Headmistress," she said. "You must have knocked it over without knowing it. That sort of thing is easy to do."

"I am fed up with you useless bunch of midgets!" roared the Trunchbull. "I refuse to waste any more of my precious time in here!" And with that she marched out of the class-room, slamming the door behind her.

In the stunned silence that followed, Miss Honey walked up to the front of the class and stood behind her table. "Phew!" she said. "I think we've had enough school for one day, don't you? The class is dismissed. You may all go out into the playground and wait for your parents to come and take you home."

The Second Miracle

Matilda did not join the rush to get out of the classroom. After the other children had all disappeared, she remained at her desk, quiet and thoughtful. She knew she had to tell somebody about what had happened with the glass. She couldn't possibly keep a gigantic secret like that bottled up inside her. What she needed was just one person, one wise and sympathetic grown-up who could help her to understand the meaning of this extraordinary happening.

Neither her mother nor her father would be of any use at all. If they believed her story, and it was doubtful they would, they almost certainly would fail to realise what an astounding event it was that had taken place in the classroom that afternoon. On the spur of the moment, Matilda decided that the one person she would like to confide in was Miss Honey.

Matilda and Miss Honey were now the only two left in the class-room. Miss Honey had seated herself at her table and was riffling through some papers. She looked up and said, "Well, Matilda, aren't you going outside with the others?"

Matilda said, "Please may I talk to you for a moment?"

"Of course you may. What's troubling you?"

"Something very peculiar has happened to me, Miss Honey."

Miss Honey became instantly alert. Ever since the two disastrous meetings she had had recently about Matilda, the first with the Headmistress and the second with the dreadful Mr and Mrs Wormwood, Miss Honey had been thinking a great deal about this child and wondering how she could help her. And now, here was Matilda sitting in the classroom with a curiously exalted look on her face and asking if she could have a private talk. Miss Honey had never seen her looking so wide-eyed and peculiar before.

"Yes, Matilda," she said. "Tell me what has happened to you that is so peculiar."

"Miss Trunchbull isn't going to expel me, is she?" Matilda asked. "Because it wasn't me who put that creature in her jug of water. I promise you it wasn't."

"I know it wasn't," Miss Honey said.

"Am I going to be expelled?"

"I think not," Miss Honey said. "The Headmistress simply got a little over-excited, that's all."

"Good," Matilda said. "But that isn't what I want to talk to you about."

"What do you want to talk to me about, Matilda?"

"I want to talk to you about the glass of water with the creature in it," Matilda said. "You saw it spilling all over Miss Trunchbull, didn't you?"

"I did indeed."

"Well, Miss Honey, I didn't touch it. I never went near it."

"I know you didn't," Miss Honey said. "You heard me telling the Headmistress that it couldn't possibly have been you."

"Ah, but it *was* me, Miss Honey," Matilda said. "That's exactly what I want to talk to you about."

Miss Honey paused and looked carefully at the child. "I don't think I quite follow you," she said.

"I got so angry at being accused of something I hadn't done that I made it happen."

"You made what happen, Matilda?"

"I made the glass tip over."

"I still don't quite understand what you mean," Miss Honey said gently.

"I did it with my eyes," Matilda said. "I was staring at it and wishing it to tip and then my eyes went all hot and funny and some sort of power came out of them and the glass just toppled over."

Miss Honey continued to look steadily at Matilda through her steel-rimmed spectacles and Matilda looked back at her just as steadily.

"I am still not following you," Miss Honey said. "Do you mean you actually willed the glass to tip over?"

"Yes," Matilda said. "With my eyes."

Miss Honey was silent for a moment. She did not think Matilda was meaning to tell a lie. It was more likely that she was simply allowing her vivid imagination to run away with her. "You mean you were sitting where you are now and you told the glass to topple over and it did?"

172

"Something like that, Miss Honey, yes."

"If you did that, then it is just about the greatest
miracle a person has ever performed since the time
of Jesus."

"I did it, Miss Honey."

It is extraordinary, thought Miss Honey, how
often small children have flights of fancy like this.
She decided to put an end to it as gently as possible.
"Could you do it again?" she asked, not unkindly.

"I don't know," Matilda said, "but I think I might
be able to."

Miss Honey moved the now empty glass to the
middle of the table. "Should I put water in it?" she
asked, smiling a little.

"I don't think it matters," Matilda said.

"Very well, then. Go ahead and tip it over."

"It may take some time."

"Take all the time you want," Miss Honey said.
"I'm in no hurry."

Matilda, sitting in the second row about ten feet away from Miss Honey, put her elbows on the desk and cupped her face in her hands, and this time she gave the order right at the beginning. *"Tip glass, tip!"* she ordered, but her lips didn't move and she made no sound. She simply shouted the words inside her head. And now she concentrated the whole of her mind and her brain and her will up into her eyes and once again but much more quickly than before she felt the electricity gathering and the power was beginning to surge and the hotness was coming into the eyeballs, and then the millions of tiny invisible arms with hands on them were shooting out towards the glass, and without making any sound at all she kept on shouting inside her head for the glass to go over. She saw it wobble, then it tilted, then it toppled right over and fell with a tinkle on to the table-top not twelve inches from Miss Honey's folded arms.

Miss Honey's mouth dropped open and her eyes stretched so wide you could see the whites all round. She didn't say a word. She couldn't. The shock of seeing the miracle performed had struck her dumb. She gaped at the glass, leaning well away from it now as though it might be a dangerous thing. Then slowly she lifted head and looked at Matilda. She saw the child white in the face, as white as paper, trembling all over, the eyes glazed, staring straight ahead and seeing nothing. The whole face was transfigured, the eyes round and bright and she was sitting there speechless, quite beautiful in a blaze of silence.

Miss Honey waited, trembling a little herself and watching the child as she slowly stirred herself back into consciousness. And then suddenly, *click* went her face into a look of almost seraphic calm. "I'm all right," she said and smiled. "I'm quite all right, Miss Honey, so don't be alarmed."

"You seemed so far away," Miss Honey whispered, awestruck.

"Oh, I was. I was flying past the stars on silver wings," Matilda said. "It was wonderful."

Miss Honey was still gazing at the child in absolute wonderment, as though she were The Creation, The Beginning Of The World, The First Morning.

"It went much quicker this time," Matilda said quietly.

"It's not possible!" Miss Honey was gasping. "I don't believe it! I simply don't believe it!" She closed her eyes and kept them closed for quite a while, and when she opened them again it seemed as though she had gathered herself together. "Would you like to come back and have tea at my cottage?" she asked.

"Oh, I'd love to," Matilda said.

"Good. Gather up your things and I'll meet you outside in a couple of minutes."

"You won't tell anyone about this . . . this thing that I did, will you, Miss Honey?"

"I wouldn't dream of it," Miss Honey said.

Miss Honey's Cottage

Miss Honey joined Matilda outside the school gates and the two of them walked in silence through the village High Street. They passed the greengrocer with his window full of apples and oranges, and the butcher with bloody lumps of meat on display and naked chickens hanging up, and the small bank, and the grocery store and the electrical shop, and then they came out at the other side of the village on to the narrow country road where there were no people any more and very few motor-cars.

And now that they were alone, Matilda all of a sudden became wildly animated. It seemed as though a valve had burst inside her and a great gush of energy was being released. She trotted beside Miss Honey with wild little hops and her fingers flew as if she would scatter them to the four winds and her words went off like fireworks, with terrific speed. It was Miss Honey this and Miss Honey that and Miss Honey I do honestly feel I could move almost anything in the world, not just tipping over glasses and little things like that . . . I feel I could topple tables and chairs, Miss Honey . . . Even when people are sitting in the chairs I think I could push them over, and bigger things too, much bigger things than chairs and tables . . . I only have to take a moment to get my eyes strong and then I can push it out, this strongness, at anything at all so long as I am staring at it hard enough . . . I have to stare at it very hard, Miss Honey, very very hard, and then I can feel it all happening behind my eyes, and my eyes get hot just as though they were burning but I don't mind that in the least, and Miss Honey . . .

"Calm yourself down, child, calm yourself down," Miss Honey said. "Let us not get ourselves too worked up so early in the proceedings."

"But you do think it is *interesting*, don't you, Miss Honey?"

"Oh, it is *interesting* all right," Miss Honey said. "It is *more* than interesting. But we must tread very carefully from now on, Matilda."

"Why must we tread carefully, Miss Honey?"

"Because we are playing with mysterious forces, my child, that we know nothing about. I do not think they are evil. They may be good. They may even be divine. But whether they are or not, let us handle them carefully."

These were wise words from a wise old bird, but Matilda was too steamed up to see it that way. "I don't see why we have to be so careful?" she said, still hopping about.

"I am trying to explain to you," Miss Honey said patiently, "that we are dealing with the unknown. It is an unexplainable thing. The right word for it is a phenomenon. It is a phenomenon."

"Am I a phenomenon?" Matilda asked.

"It is quite possible that you are," Miss Honey said. "But I'd rather you didn't think about yourself as anything in particular at the moment. What I thought we might do is to explore this phenomenon a little further, just the two of us together, but making sure we take things very carefully all the time."

"You want me to do some more of it then, Miss Honey?"

179

"That is what I am tempted to suggest," Miss Honey said cautiously.

"Goody-good," Matilda said.

"I myself," Miss Honey said, "am probably far more bowled over by what you did than you are, and I am trying to find some reasonable explanation."

"Such as what?" Matilda asked.

"Such as whether or not it's got something to do with the fact that you are quite exceptionally precocious."

"What exactly does that word mean?" Matilda said.

"A precocious child", Miss Honey said, "is one that shows amazing intelligence early on. You are an unbelievably precocious child."

"Am I really?" Matilda asked.

"Of course you are. You must be aware of that. Look at your reading. Look at your mathematics."

"I suppose you're right," Matilda said.

Miss Honey marvelled at the child's lack of conceit and self-consciousness.

"I can't help wondering", she said, "whether this sudden ability that has come to you, of being able to move an object without touching it, whether it might not have something to do with your brainpower."

"You mean there might not be room in my head for all those brains so something has to push out?"

"That's not quite what I mean," Miss Honey said, smiling. "But whatever happens, and I say it again, we must tread carefully from now on. I have not forgotten that strange and distant glimmer on your face after you tipped over the last glass."

"Do you think doing it could actually hurt me? Is that what you're thinking, Miss Honey?"

"It made you feel pretty peculiar, didn't it?"

"It made me feel lovely," Matilda said. "For a moment or two I was flying past the stars on silver wings. I told you that. And shall I tell you something else, Miss Honey? It was easier the second time, much much easier. I think it's like anything else, the more you practise it, the easier it gets."

Miss Honey was walking slowly so that the small child could keep up with her without trotting too fast, and it was very peaceful out there on the narrow road now that the village was behind them. It was one of those golden autumn afternoons and there were blackberries and splashes of old man's beard in the hedges, and the hawthorn berries were ripening scarlet for the birds when the cold winter came along. There were tall trees here and there on either side, oak and sycamore and ash and occasionally a sweet chestnut. Miss Honey, wishing to change the subject for the moment, gave the names of all these to Matilda and taught her how to recognise them by the shape of their leaves and the pattern of the bark on their trunks. Matilda took all this in and stored the knowledge away carefully in her mind.

They came finally to a gap in the hedge on the left-hand side of the road where there was a five-barred gate. "This way," Miss Honey said, and she opened the gate and led Matilda through and closed it again. They were now walking along a narrow lane that was no more than a rutted cart-track. There was a high hedge of hazel on either side and you could see clusters of ripe brown nuts in their green jackets. The squirrels would be collecting them all very soon, Miss Honey said, and storing them away carefully for the bleak months ahead.

"You mean you *live* down here?" Matilda asked.

"I do," Miss Honey replied, but she said no more.

Matilda had never once stopped to think about where Miss Honey might be living. She had always regarded her purely as a teacher, a person who turned up out of nowhere and taught at school and then went away again. Do any of us children, she wondered, ever stop to ask ourselves where our teachers go when school is over for the day? Do we wonder if they live alone, or if there is a mother at home or a sister or a husband? "Do you

live all by yourself, Miss Honey?" she asked.

"Yes," Miss Honey said. "Very much so."

They were walking over the deep sun-baked mud-tracks of the lane and you had to watch where you put your feet if you didn't want to twist your ankle. There were a few small birds around in the hazel branches but that was all.

"It's just a farm-labourer's cottage," Miss Honey said. "You mustn't expect too much of it. We're nearly there."

They came to a small green gate half-buried in the hedge on the right and almost hidden by the overhanging hazel branches. Miss Honey paused with one hand on the gate and said, "There it is. That's where I live."

Matilda saw a narrow dirt-path leading to a tiny

red-brick cottage. The cottage was so small it looked more like a doll's house than a human dwelling. The bricks it was built of were old and crumbly and very pale red. It had a grey slate roof and one small chimney, and there were two little windows at the front. Each window was no larger than a sheet of tabloid newspaper and there was clearly no upstairs to the place. On either side of the path there was a wilderness of nettles and blackberry thorns and long brown grass. An enormous oak tree stood overshadowing the cottage. Its massive spreading branches seemed to be enfolding and embracing the tiny building, and perhaps hiding it as well from the rest of the world.

Miss Honey, with one hand on the gate which she had not yet opened, turned to Matilda and said, "A poet called Dylan Thomas once wrote some lines that I think of every time I walk up this path."

Matilda waited, and Miss Honey, in a rather wonderful slow voice, began reciting the poem:

"Never and never, my girl riding far and near
In the land of the hearthstone tales, and spelled
  asleep,
Fear or believe that the wolf in the sheepwhite
  hood
Loping and bleating roughly and blithely shall
  leap, my dear, my dear,
Out of a lair in the flocked leaves in the dew
  dipped year
To eat your heart in the house in the rosy
  wood."

There was a moment of silence, and Matilda, who had never before heard great romantic poetry spoken aloud, was profoundly moved. "It's like music," she whispered.

185

"It is music," Miss Honey said. And then, as though embarrassed at having revealed such a secret part of herself, she quickly pushed open the gate and walked up the path. Matilda hung back. She was a bit frightened of this place now. It seemed so unreal and remote and fantastic and so totally away from this earth. It was like an illustration in Grimm or Hans Andersen. It was the house where the poor woodcutter lived with Hansel and Gretel and where Red Riding Hood's grandmother lived and it was also the house of The Seven Dwarfs and The Three Bears and all the rest of them. It was straight out of a fairy-tale.

"Come along, my dear," Miss Honey called back, and Matilda followed her up the path.

The front-door was covered with flaky green paint and there was no keyhole. Miss Honey simply lifted the latch and pushed open the door and went in. Although she was not a tall woman, she had to stoop low to get through the doorway. Matilda went after her and found herself in what seemed to be a dark narrow tunnel.

"You can come through to the kitchen and help me make the tea," Miss Honey said, and she led the way along the tunnel into the kitchen – that is if you could call it a kitchen. It was not much bigger than a good-sized clothes cupboard and there was one small window in the back wall with a sink under the window, but there were no taps over the sink. Against another wall there was a shelf, presumably for preparing food, and there was a single cupboard above the shelf. On the shelf itself

there stood a Primus stove, a saucepan and a half-full bottle of milk. A Primus is a little camping-stove that you fill with paraffin and you light it at the top and then you pump it to get pressure for the flame.

"You can get me some water while I light the Primus," Miss Honey said. "The well is out at the back. Take the bucket. Here it is. You'll find a rope in the well. Just hook the bucket on to the end of the rope and lower it down, but don't fall in yourself." Matilda, more bemused than ever now, took the bucket and carried it out into the back garden. The well had a little wooden roof over it and a simple winding device and there was the rope dangling down into a dark bottomless hole. Matilda pulled up the rope and hooked the handle of the bucket on to the end of it. Then she lowered it until she heard a splash and the rope went slack. She pulled it up again and lo and behold, there was water in the bucket.

"Is this enough?" she asked, carrying it in.

"Just about," Miss Honey said. "I don't suppose you've ever done that before?"

"Never," Matilda said. "It's fun. How do you get enough water for your bath?"

"I don't take a bath," Miss Honey said. "I wash standing up. I get a bucketful of water and I heat it on this little stove and I strip and wash myself all over."

"Do you honestly do that?" Matilda asked.

"Of course I do," Miss Honey said. "Every poor person in England used to wash that way until not so very long ago. And *they* didn't have a Primus. They had to heat the water over the fire in the hearth."

"Are *you* poor, Miss Honey?"

"Yes," Miss Honey said. "Very. It's a good little stove, isn't it?" The Primus was roaring away with a powerful blue flame and already the water in the saucepan was beginning to bubble. Miss Honey got a teapot from the cupboard and put some tea leaves into it. She also found half a small loaf of brown bread. She cut two thin slices and then, from a plastic container, she took some margarine and spread it on the bread.

Margarine, Matilda thought. She really must be poor.

Miss Honey found a tray and on it she put two mugs, the teapot, the half bottle of milk and a plate with the two slices of bread. "I'm afraid I don't have any sugar," she said. "I never use it."

"That's all right," Matilda said. In her wisdom she seemed to be aware of the delicacy of the situation and she was taking great care not to say anything to embarrass her companion.

189

"Let's have it in the sitting-room," Miss Honey said, picking up the tray and leading the way out of the kitchen and down the dark little tunnel into the room at the front. Matilda followed her, but just inside the doorway of the so-called sitting-room she stopped and stared around her in absolute amazement. The room was as small and square and bare as a prison cell. The pale daylight that entered came from a single tiny window in the front wall, but there were no curtains. The only objects in the entire room were two upturned wooden boxes to serve as chairs and a third box between them for a table. That was all. There were no pictures on the walls, no carpet on the floor, only rough unpolished wooden planks, and there were gaps between the planks where dust and bits of grime had gathered. The ceiling was so low that with a jump Matilda could nearly touch it with her finger-tips. The walls were white but the whiteness didn't look like paint. Matilda rubbed her palm against it and a white powder came off on to her skin. It was whitewash, the cheap stuff that is used in cowsheds and stables and hen-houses.

Matilda was appalled. Was this really where her neat and trimly-dressed school teacher lived? Was this all she had to come back to after a day's work? It was unbelievable. And what was the reason for it? There was something very strange going on around here, surely.

Miss Honey put the tray on one of the upturned boxes. "Sit down, my dear, sit down," she said, "and we'll have a nice hot cup of tea. Help yourself

190

to bread. Both slices are for you. I never eat anything when I get home. I have a good old tuck-in at the school lunch and that keeps me going until the next morning."

Matilda perched herself carefully on an upturned box and more out of politeness than anything else she took a slice of bread and margarine and started to eat it. At home she would have been having buttered toast and strawberry jam and probably a piece of sponge-cake to round it off. And yet this was somehow far more fun. There was a mystery here in this house, a great mystery, there was no doubt about that, and Matilda was longing to find out what it was.

Miss Honey poured the tea and added a little milk to both cups. She appeared to be not in the least ill at ease sitting on an upturned box in a bare room and drinking tea out of a mug that she balanced on her knee.

"You know," she said, "I've been thinking very hard about what you did with that glass. It is a great power you have been given, my child, you know that."

"Yes, Miss Honey, I do," Matilda said, chewing her bread and margarine.

"So far as I know," Miss Honey went on, "nobody else in the history of the world has been able to compel an object to move without touching it or blowing on it or using any outside help at all."

Matilda nodded but said nothing.

"The fascinating thing", Miss Honey said, "would be to find out the real limit of this power of yours. Oh, I know you think you can move just about anything there is, but I have my doubts about that."

"I'd love to try something really huge," Matilda said.

"What about distance?" Miss Honey asked. "Would you always have to be close to the thing you were pushing?"

"I simply don't know," Matilda said. "But it would be fun to find out."

Miss Honey's Story

"We mustn't hurry this," Miss Honey said, "so let's have another cup of tea. And do eat that other slice of bread. You must be hungry."

Matilda took the second slice and started eating it slowly. The margarine wasn't at all bad. She doubted whether she could have told the difference if she hadn't known. "Miss Honey," she said suddenly, "do they pay you very badly at our school?"

Miss Honey looked up sharply. "Not too badly," she said. "I get about the same as the others."

"But it must still be very little if you are so dreadfully poor," Matilda said. "Do all the teachers live like this, with no furniture and no kitchen stove and no bathroom?"

"No, they don't," Miss Honey said rather stiffly. "I just happen to be the exception."

"I expect you just happen to like living in a very simple way," Matilda said, probing a little further. "It must make house cleaning an awful lot easier and you don't have furniture to polish or any of those silly little ornaments lying around that have to be dusted every day. And I suppose if you don't have a fridge you don't have to go out and buy all sorts of junky things like eggs and mayonnaise and ice-cream to fill it up with. It must save a terrific lot of shopping."

At this point Matilda noticed that Miss Honey's face had gone all tight and peculiar-looking. Her whole body had become rigid. Her shoulders were hunched up high and her lips were pressed together tight and she sat there gripping her mug of tea in both hands and staring down into it as though searching for a way to answer these not-quite-so-innocent questions.

There followed a rather long and embarrassing silence. In the space of thirty seconds the atmosphere in the tiny room had changed completely and now it was vibrating with awkwardness and secrets. Matilda said, "I am very sorry I asked you

those questions, Miss Honey. It is not any of my business."

At this, Miss Honey seemed to rouse herself. She gave a shake of her shoulders and then very carefully she placed her mug on the tray.

"Why shouldn't you ask?" she said. "You were bound to ask in the end. You are much too bright not to have wondered. Perhaps I even *wanted* you to ask. Maybe that is why I invited you here after all. As a matter of fact you are the first visitor to come to the cottage since I moved in two years ago."

Matilda said nothing. She could feel the tension growing and growing in the room.

"You are so much wiser than your years, my dear," Miss Honey went on, "that it quite staggers me. Although you look like a child, you are not really a child at all because your mind and your powers of reasoning seem to be fully grown-up. So I suppose we might call you a grown-up child, if you see what I mean."

Matilda still did not say anything. She was waiting for what was coming next.

"Up to now", Miss Honey went on, "I have found it impossible to talk to anyone about my problems. I couldn't face the embarrassment, and anyway I lack the courage. Any courage I had was knocked out of me when I was young. But now, all of a sudden I have a sort of desperate wish to tell everything to somebody. I know you are only a tiny little girl, but there is some kind of magic in you somewhere. I've seen it with my own eyes."

Matilda became very alert. The voice she was hearing was surely crying out for help. It must be. It had to be.

Then the voice spoke again. "Have some more tea," it said. "I think there's still a drop left."

Matilda nodded.

Miss Honey poured tea into both mugs and added milk. Again she cupped her own mug in both hands and sat there sipping.

There was quite a long silence before she said, "May I tell you a story?"

"Of course," Matilda said.

"I am twenty-three years old," Miss Honey said, "and when I was born my father was a doctor in this village. We had a nice old house, quite large, red-brick. It's tucked away in the woods behind the hills. I don't think you'd know it."

Matilda kept silent.

"I was born there," Miss Honey said. "And then came the first tragedy. My mother died when I was two. My father, a busy doctor, had to have someone to run the house and to look after me. So he invited my mother's unmarried sister, my aunt, to come and live with us. She agreed and she came."

Matilda was listening intently. "How old was the aunt when she moved in?" she asked.

"Not very old," Miss Honey said. "I should say about thirty. But I hated her right from the start. I missed my mother terribly. And the aunt was not a kind person. My father didn't know that because he was hardly every around but when he did put in an appearance, the aunt behaved differently."

Miss Honey paused and sipped her tea. "I can't think why I am telling you all this," she said, embarrassed.

"Go on," Matilda said. "Please."

"Well," Miss Honey said, "then came the second tragedy. When I was five, my father died very suddenly. One day he was there and the next day he was gone. And so I was left to live alone with my aunt. She became my legal guardian. She had all the powers of a parent over me. And in some way or another, she became the actual owner of the house."

"How did your father die?" Matilda asked.

"It is interesting you should ask that," Miss Honey said. "I myself was much too young to question it at the time, but I found out later that there was a good deal of mystery surrounding his death."

"Didn't they know how he died?" Matilda asked.

"Well, not exactly," Miss Honey said, hesitating, "You see, no one could believe that he would ever have done it. He was such a very sane and sensible man."

"Done what?" Matilda asked.

"*Killed* himself."

Matilda was stunned.
"Did he?" she
gasped.

"That's what it *looked* like," Miss Honey said. "But who knows?" She shrugged and turned away and stared out of the tiny window.

"I know what you're thinking," Matilda said. "You're thinking that the aunt killed him and made it look as though he'd done it himself."

"I am not thinking anything," Miss Honey said. "One must never think things like that without proof."

The little room became quiet. Matilda noticed that the hands clasping the mug were trembling slightly. "What happened after that?" she asked. "What happened when you were left all alone with the aunt? Wasn't she nice to you?"

"Nice?" Miss Honey said. "She was a demon. As soon as my father was out of the way she became a holy terror. My life was a nightmare."

"What did she do to you?" Matilda asked.

"I don't want to talk about it," Miss Honey said. "It's too horrible. But in the end I became so frightened of her I used to start shaking when she came into the room. You must understand I was never a strong character like you. I was always shy and retiring."

"Didn't you have any other relations?" Matilda asked. "Any uncles or aunts or grannies who would come and see you?"

"None that I knew about," Miss Honey said. "They were all either dead or they'd gone to Australia. And that's still the way it is now, I'm afraid."

"So you grew up in that house alone with your

198

aunt," Matilda said. "But you must have gone to school."

"Of course," Miss Honey said. "I went to the same school you're going to now. But I lived at home." Miss Honey paused and stared down into her empty tea-mug. "I think what I am trying to explain to you," she said, "is that over the years I became so completely cowed and dominated by this monster of an aunt that when she gave me an order, no matter what it was, I obeyed it instantly. That can happen, you know. And by the time I was ten, I had become her slave. I did all the housework. I made her bed. I washed and ironed for her. I did all the cooking. I learned how to do everything."

"But surely you could have complained to *somebody*?" Matilda said.

"To whom?" Miss Honey said. "And anyway, I was far too terrified to complain. I told you, I was her slave."

"Did she beat you?"

"Let's not go into details," Miss Honey said.

"How simply *awful*," Matilda said. "Did you cry nearly all the time?"

"Only when I was alone," Miss Honey said. "I wasn't allowed to cry in front of her. But I lived in fear."

"What happened when you left school?" Matilda asked.

"I was a bright pupil," Miss Honey said. "I could easily have got into university. But there was no question of that."

"Why not, Miss Honey?"

"Because I was needed at home to do the work."

"Then how did you become a teacher?" Matilda asked.

"There is a Teacher's Training College in Reading," Miss Honey said. "That's only forty minutes' bus-ride away from here. I was allowed to go there on condition I came straight home again every afternoon to do the washing and ironing and to clean the house and cook the supper."

"How old were you then?" Matilda asked.

"When I went into Teacher's Training I was eighteen," Miss Honey said.

"You could have just packed up and walked away," Matilda said.

"Not until I got a job," Miss Honey said. "And don't forget, I was by then dominated by my aunt to such an extent that I wouldn't have dared. You can't imagine what it's like to be completely controlled like that by a very strong personality. It turns you to jelly. So that's it. That's the sad story of my life. Now I've talked enough."

"Please don't stop," Matilda said. "You haven't finished yet. How did you manage to get away from her in the end and come and live in this funny little house?"

"Ah, that was something," Miss Honey said. "I was proud of that."

"Tell me," Matilda said.

"Well," Miss Honey said, "when I got my teacher's job, the aunt told me I owed her a lot of money. I asked her why. She said, 'Because I've been feeding you for all these years and buying

200

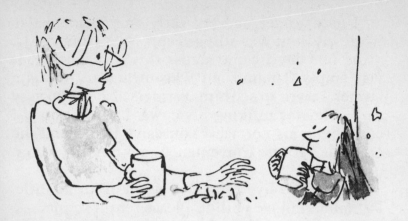

your shoes and your clothes!' She told me it added
up to thousands and I had to pay her back by giving
her my salary for the next ten years. 'I'll give you
one pound a week pocket-money,' she said. 'But
that's all you're going to get.' She even arranged
with the school authorities to have my salary paid
directly into her own bank. She made me sign the
paper."

"You shouldn't have done that," Matilda said.
"Your salary was your chance of freedom."

"I know, I know," Miss Honey said. "But by then
I had been her slave nearly all my life and I hadn't
the courage or the guts to say no. I was still petrified
of her. She could still hurt me badly."

"So how did you manage to escape?" Matilda
asked.

"Ah," Miss Honey said, smiling for the first
time, "that was two years ago. It was my greatest
triumph."

"Please tell me," Matilda said.

"I used to get up very early and go for walks while my aunt was still asleep," Miss Honey said. "And one day I came across this tiny cottage. It was empty. I found out who owned it. It was a farmer. I went to see him. Farmers also get up very early. He was milking his cows. I asked him if I could rent his cottage. 'You can't live there!' he cried. 'It's got no conveniences, no running water, no nothing!'"

" 'I want to live there,' I said. 'I'm a romantic. I've fallen in love with it. Please rent it to me.'

" 'You're mad,' he said. 'But if you insist, you're welcome to it. The rent will be ten pence a week.'

" 'Here's one month's rent in advance,' I said, giving him 40p. 'And thank you so much!'"

"How super!" Matilda cried. "So suddenly you had a house all of your own! But how did you pluck up the courage to tell the aunt?"

"That was tough," Miss Honey said. "But I steeled myself to do it. One night, after I had cooked her supper, I went upstairs and packed the few things I possessed in a cardboard box and came downstairs and announced I was leaving. 'I've rented a house,' I said.

"My aunt exploded. 'Rented a house!' she shouted. 'How can you rent a house when you have only one pound a week in the world?'

" 'I've done it,' I said.

" 'And how are you going to buy food for yourself?'

" 'I'll manage,' I mumbled and rushed out of the front door."

202

"Oh, well done you!" Matilda cried. "So you were free at last!"

"I was free at last," Miss Honey said. "I can't tell you how wonderful it was."

"But have you really managed to live here on one pound a week for two years?" Matilda asked.

"I most certainly have," Miss Honey said. "I pay ten pence rent, and the rest just about buys me paraffin for my stove and for my lamp, and a little milk and tea and bread and margarine. That's all I need really. As I told you, I have a jolly good tuck-in at the school lunch."

Matilda stared at her. What a marvellously brave thing Miss Honey had done. Suddenly she was a heroine in Matilda's eyes. "Isn't it awfully cold in the winter?" she asked.

"I've got my little paraffin stove," Miss Honey said. "You'd be surprised how snug I can make it in here."

"Do you have a bed, Miss Honey?"

"Well not exactly," Miss Honey said, smiling again. "But they say it's very healthy to sleep on a hard surface."

All at once Matilda was able to see the whole situation with absolute clarity. Miss Honey needed help. There was no way she could go on existing like this indefinitely. "You would be a lot better off, Miss Honey," she said, "if you gave up your job and drew unemployment money."

"I would never do that," Miss Honey said. "I love teaching."

"This awful aunt," Matilda said, "I suppose she is still living in your lovely old house?"

"Very much so," Miss Honey said. "She's still only about fifty. She'll be around for a long time yet."

"And do you think your father really meant her to own the house for ever?"

"I'm quite sure he didn't," Miss Honey said. "Parents will often give a guardian the right to occupy the house for a certain length of time, but it is nearly always left in trust for the child. It then becomes the child's property when he or she grows up."

"Then surely it is your house?" Matilda said.

"My father's will was never found," Miss Honey said. "It looks as though somebody destroyed it."

"No prizes for guessing who," Matilda said.

"No prizes," Miss Honey said.

"But if there is no will, Miss Honey, then surely the house goes automatically to you. You are the next of kin."

"I know I am," Miss Honey said. "But my aunt produced a piece of paper supposedly written by my father saying that he leaves the house to his sister-in-law in return for her kindness in looking after me. I am certain it's a forgery. But no one can prove it."

"Couldn't you try?" Matilda said. "Couldn't you hire a good lawyer and make a fight of it."

"I don't have the money to do that," Miss Honey said. "And you must remember that this aunt of mine is a much respected figure in the community. She has a lot of influence."

"Who is she?" Matilda asked.

Miss Honey hesitated a moment. Then she said softly, "Miss Trunchbull."

The Names

"Miss Trunchbull!" Matilda cried, jumping about a foot in the air. "You mean *she* is your aunt? *She* brought you up?"

"Yes," Miss Honey said.

"No *wonder* you were terrified!" Matilda cried. "The other day we saw her grab a girl by the pigtails and throw her over the playground fence!"

"You haven't seen anything," Miss Honey said. "After my father died, when I was five and a half, she used to make me bath myself all alone. And if she came up and thought I hadn't washed properly she would push my head under the water and hold it there. But don't get me started on what she used to do. That won't help us at all."

"No," Matilda said, "it won't."

"We came here", Miss Honey said," to talk about *you* and I've been talking about nothing but myself the whole time. I feel like a fool. I am much more interested in just how much you can do with those amazing eyes of yours."

"I can move things," Matilda said. "I know I can. I can push things over."

"How would you like it", Miss Honey said, "if we made some very cautious experiments to see just how much you can move and push?"

Quite surprisingly, Matilda said, "If you don't

mind, Miss Honey, I think I would rather not. I want to go home now and think and think about all the things I've heard this afternoon."

Miss Honey stood up at once. "Of course," she said. "I have kept you here far too long. Your mother will be starting to worry."

"She never does that," Matilda said, smiling. "But I would like to go home now please, if you don't mind."

"Come along then," Miss Honey said. "I'm sorry I gave you such a rotten tea."

"You didn't at all," Matilda said. "I loved it."

The two of them walked all the way to Matilda's house in complete silence. Miss Honey sensed that Matilda wanted it that way. The child seemed so lost in thought she hardly looked where she was walking, and when they reached the gate of Matilda's home, Miss Honey said, "You had better forget everything I told you this afternoon."

"I won't promise to do that," Matilda said, "but I will promise not to talk about it to anyone any more, not even to you."

"I think that would be wise," Miss Honey said.

"I won't promise to stop thinking about it, though, Miss Honey," Matilda said. "I've been thinking about it all the way back from your cottage and I believe I've got just a tiny little bit of an idea."

"You mustn't," Miss Honey said. "Please forget it."

"I would like to ask you three last things before

I stop talking about it," Matilda said. "Please will you answer them, Miss Honey?"

Miss Honey smiled. It was extraordinary, she told herself, how this little snippet of a girl seemed suddenly to be taking charge of her problems, and with such authority, too. "Well," she said, "that depends on what the questions are."

"The first thing is this," Matilda said. "What did Miss Trunchbull call *your father* when they were around the house at home?"

"I'm sure she called him Magnus," Miss Honey said. "That was his first name."

"And what did your father call Miss Trunchbull?"

"Her name is Agatha," Miss Honey said. "That's what he would have called her."

"And lastly," Matilda said, "what did your father and Miss Trunchbull call *you* around the house?"

"They called me Jenny," Miss Honey said.

Matilda pondered these answers very carefully. "Let me make sure I've got them right," she said. "In the house at home, your father was Magnus, Miss Trunchbull was Agatha and you were Jenny. Am I right?"

"That is correct," Miss Honey said.

"Thank you," Matilda said. "And now I won't mention the subject any more."

Miss Honey wondered what on earth was going on in the mind of this child. "Don't do anything silly," she said.

Matilda laughed and turned away and ran up the path to her front-door, calling out as she went, "Good-bye, Miss Honey! Thank you so much for the tea."

The Practice

Matilda found the house empty as usual. Her father was not yet back from work, her mother was not yet back from bingo and her brother might be anywhere. She went straight into the living-room and opened the drawer of the sideboard where she knew her father kept a box of cigars. She took one out and carried it up to her bedroom and shut herself in.

Now for the practice, she told herself. It's going to be tough but I'm determined to do it.

Her plan for helping Miss Honey was beginning to form beautifully in her mind. She had it now in almost every detail, but in the end it all depended upon her being able to do one very special thing with her eye-power. She knew she wouldn't manage it right away, but she felt fairly confident that with a great deal of practice and effort, she would succeed in the end. The cigar was essential. It was perhaps a bit thicker than she would have liked, but the weight was about right. It would be fine for practising with.

There was a small dressing-table in Matilda's bedroom with her hairbrush and comb on it and two library books. She cleared these things to one side and laid the cigar down in the middle of the dressing-table. Then she walked away and sat on

the end of her bed. She was now about ten feet
from the cigar.

She settled herself and began to concentrate,
and very quickly this time she felt the electricity
beginning to flow inside her head, gathering itself
behind the eyes, and the eyes became hot and
millions of tiny invisible hands began pushing out
like sparks towards the cigar. "Move!" she whispered, and to her intense surprise, almost at once,
the cigar with its little red and gold paper band
around its middle rolled away across the top of the
dressing-table and fell on to the carpet.

Matilda had enjoyed that. It was lovely doing it. It had felt as though sparks were going round and round inside her head and flashing out of her eyes. It had given her a sense of power that was almost ethereal. And how quick it had been this time! How simple!

She crossed the bedroom and picked up the cigar and put it back on the table.

Now for the difficult one, she thought. But if I have the power to *push*, then surely I also have the power to *lift*? It is *vital* I learn how to lift it. I *must* learn how to lift it right up into the air and keep it there. It is not a very heavy thing, a cigar.

She sat on the end of the bed and started again. It was easy now to summon up the power behind her eyes. It was like pushing a trigger in the brain. *"Lift!"* she whispered. *"Lift! Lift!"*

At first the cigar started to roll away. But then, with Matilda concentrating fiercely, one end of it slowly lifted up about an inch off the table-top.

With a colossal effort, she managed to hold it there for about ten seconds. Then it fell back again.

"Phew!" she gasped. "I'm getting it! I'm starting to do it!"

For the next hour, Matilda kept practising, and in the end she had managed, by the sheer power of her eyes, to lift the whole cigar clear off the table

about six inches into the air and hold it there for about a minute. Then suddenly she was so exhausted she fell back on the bed and went to sleep.

That was how her mother found her later in the evening.

"What's the matter with you?" the mother said, waking her up. "Are you ill?"

"Oh gosh," Matilda said, sitting up and looking around. "No. I'm all right. I was a bit tired, that's all."

From then on, every day after school, Matilda shut herself in her room and practised with the cigar. And soon it all began to come together in the most wonderful way. Six days later, by the following Wednesday evening, she was able not only to lift the cigar up into the air but also to move it around exactly as she wished. It was beautiful. "I can do it!" she cried. "I can really do it! I can pick the cigar up just with my eye-power and push it and pull it in the air any way I want!"

All she had to do now was to put her great plan into action.

The Third Miracle

The next day was Thursday, and that, as the whole of Miss Honey's class knew, was the day on which the Headmistress would take charge of the first lesson after lunch.

In the morning Miss Honey said to them, "One or two of you did not particularly enjoy the last occasion when the Headmistress took the class, so let us all try to be especially careful and clever today. How are your ears, Eric, after your last encounter with Miss Trunchbull?"

"She stretched them," Eric said. "My mother said she's positive they are bigger than they were."

"And Rupert," Miss Honey said, "I am glad to see you didn't lose any of your hair after last Thursday."

"My head was jolly sore afterwards," Rupert said.

"And you, Nigel," Miss Honey said, "do please try not to be smart-aleck with the Headmistress today. You were really quite cheeky to her last week."

"I hate her," Nigel said.

"Try not to make it so obvious," Miss Honey said. "It doesn't pay. She's a very strong woman. She has muscles like steel ropes."

"I wish I was grown up," Nigel said. "I'd knock her flat."

"I doubt you would," Miss Honey said. "No one has ever got the better of her yet."

"What will she be testing us on this afternoon?" a small girl asked.

"Almost certainly the three-times table," Miss Honey said. "That's what you are all meant to have learnt this past week. Make sure you know it."

Lunch came and went.

After lunch, the class reassembled. Miss Honey stood at one side of the room. They all sat silent, apprehensive, waiting. And then, like some giant of doom, the enormous Trunchbull strode into the room in her green breeches and cotton smock. She went straight to her jug of water and lifted it up by the handle and peered inside.

"I am glad to see", she said, "that there are no slimy creatures in my drinking-water this time. If there had been, then something exceptionally unpleasant would have happened to every single member of this class. And that includes you, Miss Honey."

The class remained silent and very tense. They had learnt a bit about this tigress by now and nobody was about to take any chances.

"Very well," boomed the Trunchbull. "Let us see how well you know your three-times table. Or to put it another way, let us see how badly Miss Honey has taught you the three-times table." The Trunchbull was standing in front of the class, legs apart, hands on hips, scowling at Miss Honey who stood silent to one side.

Matilda, sitting motionless at her desk in the

216

second row, was watching things very closely.

"You!" the Trunchbull shouted, pointing a finger the size of a rolling-pin at a boy called Wilfred. Wilfred was on the extreme right of the front row. "Stand up, you!" she shouted at him.

Wilfred stood up.

"Recite the three-times table backwards!" the Trunchbull barked.

"Backwards?" stammered Wilfred. "But I haven't learnt it backwards."

"There you are!" cried the Trunchbull, triumphant. "She's taught you nothing! Miss Honey, why have you taught them absolutely nothing at all in the last week?"

"That is not true, Headmistress," Miss Honey said. "They have all learnt their three-times table. But I see no point in teaching it to them backwards. There is little point in teaching anything backwards. The whole object of life, Headmistress, is to go forwards. I venture to ask whether even you, for example, can spell a simple word like *wrong* backwards straight away. I very much doubt it."

"Don't you get impertinent with me, Miss Honey!" the Trunchbull snapped, then she turned back to the unfortunate Wilfred. "Very well, boy," she said. "Answer me this. I have seven apples, seven oranges and seven bananas. How many pieces of fruit do I have altogether? Hurry up! Get on with it! Give me the answer!"

"That's *adding up!*" Wilfred cried. "That isn't the three-times table!"

"You blithering idiot!" shouted the Trunchbull.

"You festering gumboil! You fleabitten fungus! That *is* the three-times table! You have three separate lots of fruit and each lot has seven pieces. Three sevens are twenty-one. Can't you see that, you stagnant cesspool! I'll give you one more chance. I have eight coconuts, eight monkey-nuts and eight nutty little idiots like you. How many nuts do I have altogether? Answer me quickly."

Poor Wilfred was properly flustered. "Wait!" he cried. "Please wait! I've got to add up eight coconuts and eight monkey-nuts . . . " He started counting on his fingers.

"You bursting blister!" yelled the Trunchbull. "You moth-eaten maggot! This is *not* adding up! This is multiplication! The answer is three eights! Or is it eight threes? What is the difference between three eights and eight threes? Tell me that, you mangled little wurzel and look sharp about it!"

By now Wilfred was far too frightened and bewildered even to speak.

In two strides the Trunchbull was beside him, and by some amazing gymnastic trick, it may have been judo or karate, she flipped the back of Wilfred's legs with one of her feet so that the boy shot up off the ground and turned a somersault in the air. But halfway through the somersault she caught him by an ankle and held him dangling upside-down like a plucked chicken in a shop-window.

"Eight threes," the Trunchbull shouted, swinging Wilfred from side to side by his ankle, "eight

threes is the same as three eights and three eights
are twenty-four! Repeat that!"

At exactly that moment Nigel, at the other end
of the room, jumped to his feet and started pointing
excitedly at the blackboard and screaming, "The
chalk! The chalk! Look at the chalk! It's moving
all on its own!"

So hysterical and shrill was Nigel's scream that everyone in the place, including the Trunchbull, looked up at the blackboard. And there, sure enough, a brand-new piece of chalk was hovering near the grey-black writing surface of the blackboard.

"*It's writing something!*" screamed Nigel. "*The chalk is writing something!*"

And indeed it was.

"*What the blazes is this?*" yelled the Trunchbull. It had shaken her to see her own first name being written like that by an invisible hand. She dropped Wilfred on to the floor. Then she yelled at nobody in particular, "Who's *doing* this? Who's *writing* it?"

The chalk continued to write.

Agatha, this is Magnus
This is Magnus

Everyone in the place heard the gasp that came from the Trunchbull's throat. "No!" she cried, "It can't be! It can't be Magnus!"

It _is_ Magnus
And you'd better
believe it

Miss Honey, at the side of the room glanced swiftly at Matilda. The child was sitting very straight at her desk, the head held high, the mouth compressed, the eyes glittering like two stars.

221

Agatha, give my Jenny back her house

For some reason everyone now looked at the Trunchbull. The woman's face had turned white as snow and her mouth was opening and shutting like a halibut out of water and giving out a series of strangled gasps.

> Give my Jenny her wages
> Give my Jenny the house
> Then get out of here.
> If you don't, I will come
>   and get you
> I will come and get you
> like you got me.
> I am watching you
>   Agatha.

The chalk stopped writing. It hovered for a few moments, then suddenly it dropped to the floor with a tinkle and broke in two.

Wilfred, who had managed to resume his seat in the front row, screamed, "Miss Trunchbull has fallen down! Miss Trunchbull is on the floor!"

This was the most sensational bit of news of all and the entire class jumped up out of their seats to have a really good look. And there she was, the huge figure of the Headmistress, stretched full-length on her back across the floor, out for the count.

Miss Honey ran forward and knelt beside the prostrate giant. "She's fainted!" she cried. "She's out cold! Someone go and fetch the matron at once." Three children ran out of the room.

Nigel, always ready for action, leapt up and seized the big jug of water. "My father says cold water is the best way to wake up someone who's fainted," he said, and with that he tipped the entire contents of the jug over the Trunchbull's head. No one, not even Miss Honey, protested.

As for Matilda, she continued to sit motionless at her desk. She was feeling curiously elated. She felt as though she had touched something that was not quite of this world, the highest point of the heavens, the farthest star. She had felt most wonderfully the power surging up behind her eyes, gushing like a warm fluid inside her skull, and her eyes had become scorching hot, hotter than ever before, and things had come bursting out of her eye-sockets and then the piece of chalk had lifted itself up and had begun to write. It seemed as though she had hardly done anything, it had all been so simple.

The school matron, followed by five teachers, three women and two men, came rushing into the room.

"By golly, somebody's floored her at last!" cried one of the men, grinning. "Congratulations, Miss Honey!"

"Who threw the water over her?" asked the matron.

"I did," said Nigel proudly.

"Good for you," another teacher said. "Shall we get some more?"

"Stop that," the matron said. "We must carry her up to the sick-room."

It took all five teachers and the matron to lift the enormous woman and stagger with her out of the room.

Miss Honey said to the class, "I think you'd all better go out to the playground and amuse yourselves until the next lesson." Then she turned and walked over to the blackboard and carefully wiped out all the chalk writing.

The children began filing out of the classroom. Matilda started to go with them, but as she passed Miss Honey she paused and her twinkling eyes met the teacher's eyes and Miss Honey ran forward and gave the tiny child a great big hug and a kiss.

A New Home

Later that day, the news began to spread that the Headmistress had recovered from her fainting-fit and had then marched out of the school building tight-lipped and white in the face.

The next morning she did not turn up at school. At lunchtime, Mr Trilby, the Deputy Head, telephoned her house to enquire if she was feeling unwell. There was no answer to the phone.

When school was over, Mr Trilby decided to investigate further, so he walked to the house where Miss Trunchbull lived on the edge of the village, the lovely small red-brick Georgian building known as The Red House, tucked away in the woods behind the hills.

He rang the bell. No answer.

He knocked loudly. No answer.

He called out, "Is anybody at home?" No answer.

He tried the door and to his surprise found it unlocked. He went in.

The house was silent and there was no one in it, and yet all the furniture was still in place. Mr Trilby went upstairs to the main bedroom. Here also everything seemed to be normal until he started opening drawers and looking into cupboards. There were no clothes or underclothes or shoes anywhere. They had all gone.

She's done a bunk, Mr Trilby said to himself and he went away to inform the School Governors that the Headmistress had apparently vanished.

On the second morning, Miss Honey received by registered post a letter from a firm of local solicitors informing her that the last will and testament of her late father, Dr Honey, had suddenly and mysteriously turned up. This document revealed that ever since her father's death, Miss Honey had in fact been the rightful owner of a property on the edge of the village known as The Red House, which until recently had been occupied by a Miss Agatha Trunchbull. The will also showed that her father's lifetime savings, which fortunately were still safely in the bank, had also been left to her. The solicitor's letter added that if Miss Honey would kindly call in to the office as soon as possible, then the property and the money could be transferred into her name very rapidly.

Miss Honey did just that, and within a couple of weeks she had moved into The Red House, the very place in which she had been brought up and where luckily all the family furniture and pictures were still around. From then on, Matilda was a welcome visitor to The Red House every single evening after school, and a very close friendship began to develop between the teacher and the small child.

Back at school, great changes were also taking place. As soon as it became clear that Miss Trunchbull had completely disappeared from the scene, the excellent Mr Trilby was appointed Head Teacher in her place. And very soon after that,

Matilda was moved up into the top form where Miss Plimsoll quickly discovered that this amazing child was every bit as bright as Miss Honey had said.

One evening a few weeks later, Matilda was having tea with Miss Honey in the kitchen of The Red House after school as they always did, when Matilda said suddenly, "Something strange has happened to me, Miss Honey."

"Tell me about it," Miss Honey said.

"This morning," Matilda said, "just for fun I tried to push something over with my eyes and I couldn't do it. Nothing moved. I didn't even feel the hotness building up behind my eyeballs. The power had gone. I think I've lost it completely."

Miss Honey carefully buttered a slice of brown bread and put a little strawberry jam on it. "I've been expecting something like that to happen," she said.

"You have? Why?" Matilda asked.

"Well," Miss Honey said, "it's only a guess, but here's what I think. While you were in my class you had nothing to do, nothing to make you struggle. Your fairly enormous brain was going crazy with frustration. It was bubbling and boiling away like mad inside your head. There was tremendous energy bottled up in there with nowhere to go, and somehow or other you were able to shoot that energy out through your eyes and make objects move. But now things are different. You are in the top form competing against children more than twice your age and all that mental energy is being

used up in class. Your brain is for the first time having to struggle and strive and keep really busy, which is great. That's only a theory, mind you, and it may be a silly one, but I don't think it's far off the mark."

"I'm glad it's happened," Matilda said. "I wouldn't want to go through life as a miracle-worker."

"You've done enough," Miss Honey said. "I can still hardly believe you made all this happen for me."

Matilda, who was perched on a tall stool at the kitchen table, ate her bread and jam slowly. She did so love these afternoons with Miss Honey. She felt completely comfortable in her presence, and the two of them talked to each other more or less as equals.

"Did you know", Matilda said suddenly, "that the heart of a mouse beats at the rate of *six hundred and fifty times a second*?"

"I did not," Miss Honey said smiling. "How absolutely fascinating. Where did you read that?"

"In a book from the library," Matilda said. "And that mean it goes so fast you can't even hear the separate beats. It must sound just like a buzz."

"It must," Miss Honey said.

"And how fast do you think a hedgehog's heart beats?" Matilda asked.

"Tell me," Miss Honey said, smiling again.

"It's not as fast as a mouse," Matilda said. "It's three hundred times a minute. But even so, you wouldn't have thought it went as fast as that in a creature that moves so slowly, would you, Miss Honey?"

"I certainly wouldn't," Miss Honey said. "Tell me one more."

"A horse," Matilda said. "That's really slow. It's only forty times a minute."

This child, Miss Honey told herself, seems to be interested in everything. When one is with her it is impossible to be bored. I love it.

The two of them stayed sitting and talking in the kitchen for an hour or so longer, and then, at about six o'clock, Matilda said goodnight and set out to walk home to her parent's house, which was about an eight-minute journey away. When she arrived at her own gate, she saw a large black

Mercedes motor-car parked outside. She didn't take too much notice of that. There were often strange cars parked outside her father's place. But when she entered the house, she was confronted by a scene of utter chaos. Her mother and father were both in the hall frantically stuffing clothing and various objects into suitcases.

"What on earth's going on?" she cried. "What's happening, daddy?"

"We're off," Mr Wormwood said, not looking up. "We're leaving for the airport in half an hour so you'd better get packed. Your brother's upstairs all ready to go. Get a move on, girl! Get going!"

"Off?" Matilda cried out. "Where to?"

"Spain," the father said. "It's a better climate than this lousy country."

"Spain!" Matilda cried. "I don't want to go to Spain! I love it here and I love my school!"

"Just do as you're told and stop arguing," the father snapped. "I've got enough troubles without messing about with you!"

"But daddy . . . " Matilda began.

"Shut up!" the father shouted. "We're leaving in thirty minutes! I'm not missing that plane!"

"But how long for, daddy?" Matilda cried. "When are we coming back?"

"We aren't," the father said. "Now beat it! I'm busy!"

Matilda turned away from him and walked out through the open front-door. As soon as she was on the road she began to run. She headed straight back towards Miss Honey's house and she reached it in less than four minutes. She flew up the drive and suddenly she saw Miss Honey in the front garden, standing in the middle of a bed of roses doing something with a pair of clippers. Miss Honey had heard the sound of Matilda's feet racing

over the gravel and now she straightened up and turned and stepped out of the rose-bed as the child came running up.

"My, my!" she said. "What in the world is the matter?"

Matilda stood before her, panting, out of breath, her small face flushed crimson all over.

"They're *leaving*!" she cried. "They've all gone mad and they're filling their suitcases and they're leaving for Spain in about thirty minutes!"

"Who is?" Miss Honey asked quietly.

"Mummy and daddy and my brother Mike and they say I've got to go with them!"

"You mean for a holiday?" Miss Honey asked.

"For *ever*!" Matilda cried. "Daddy said we were *never* coming back!"

There was a brief silence, then Miss Honey said, "Actually I'm not very surprised."

"You mean you *knew* they were going?" Matilda cried. "Why didn't you tell me?"

"No, darling," Miss Honey said. "I did not know they were going. But the news still doesn't surprise me."

"Why?" Matilda cried. "Please tell me why." She was still out of breath from the running and from the shock of it all.

"Because your father", Miss Honey said, "is in with a bunch of crooks. Everyone in the village knows that. My guess is that he is a receiver of stolen cars from all over the country. He's in it deep."

Matilda stared at her open-mouthed.

Miss Honey went on, "People brought stolen cars to your father's workshop where he changed the number-plates and resprayed the bodies a different colour and all the rest of it. And now somebody's probably tipped him off that the police are on to him and he's doing what they all do, running off to Spain where they can't get him. He'll have been sending his money out there for years, all ready and waiting for him to arrive."

They were standing on the lawn in front of the lovely red-brick house with its weathered old red tiles and its tall chimneys, and Miss Honey still had the pair of garden clippers in one hand. It was a warm golden evening and a blackbird was singing somewhere near by.

"I don't want to go with them!" Matilda shouted suddenly. "I won't go with them."

"I'm afraid you must," Miss Honey said.

"I want to live here with you," Matilda cried out. "Please let me live here with you!"

"I only wish you could," Miss Honey said. "But I'm afraid it's not possible. You cannot leave your parents just because you want to. They have a right to take you with them."

"But what if they agreed?" Matilda cried eagerly. "What if they said yes, I can stay with you? Would you let me stay with you then?"

Miss Honey said softly, "Yes, that would be heaven."

"Well, I think they might!" Matilda cried. "I honestly think they might! They don't actually care tuppence about me!"

"Not so fast," Miss Honey said.

"We've got to be fast!" Matilda cried. "They're leaving any moment! Come on!" she shouted, grasping Miss Honey's hand. "Please come with me and ask them! But we'll have to hurry! We'll have to run!"

The next moment the two of them were running down the drive together and then out on to the road, and Matilda was ahead, pulling Miss Honey after her by her wrist, and it was a wild and wonderful dash they made along the country lane and through the village to the house where Matilda's parents lived. The big black Mercedes was still outside and now its boot and all its doors were open and Mr and Mrs Wormwood and the brother were scurrying around it like ants, piling in the suitcases, as Matilda and Miss Honey came dashing up.

"Daddy and mummy!" Matilda burst out, gasping for breath. "I don't want to go with you! I want to stay here and live with Miss Honey and she says that I can but only if you give me permission! Please say yes! Go on, daddy, say yes! Say yes, mummy!"

The father turned and looked at Miss Honey. "You're that teacher woman who once came here

to see me, aren't you?" he said. Then he went back to stowing the suitcases into the car.

His wife said to him, "This one'll have to go on the back seat. There's no more room in the boot."

"I would love to have Matilda," Miss Honey said. "I would look after her with loving care, Mr Wormwood, and I would pay for everything. She wouldn't cost you a penny. But it was not my idea. It was Matilda's. And I will not agree to take her without your full and willing consent."

"Come on, Harry," the mother said, pushing a suitcase into the back seat. "Why don't we let her go if that's what she wants. It'll be one less to look after."

"I'm in a hurry," the father said. "I've got a plane

to catch. If she wants to stay, let her stay. It's fine with me."

Matilda leapt into Miss Honey's arms and hugged her, and Miss Honey hugged her back, and then the mother and father and brother were inside the car and the car was pulling away with the tyres screaming. The brother gave a wave through the rear window, but the other two didn't even look back. Miss Honey was still hugging the tiny girl in her arms and neither of them said a word as they stood there watching the big black car tearing round the corner at the end of the road and disappearing for ever into the distance.